The Liberty Song

Come join hand in hand, brave Americans all,
And rouse your bold hearts at fair Liberty's call;
No tyrannous acts shall suppress your just claim,
Or stain with dishonor America's name.

Our worthy forefathers, let's give 'em a cheer,
To climates unknown did courageously steer,
Thro' oceans to deserts for freedom they come,
And dying bequeath'd their freedom and fame.

Samuel Adams

1767

Meetings

As Tucks strode along the wharf, he had one thought in mind—being alone with the sea and the sun. As he neared his favorite place on Gregson's Wharf, he saw a large stack of crates where he usually sat, and then a rope ladder with some child climbing down it. Tucks was angry and shouted, "What be you doing on those crates? Do not you know that cargo is no place to play? What were your folks thinking, letting you roam the docks? Why be you not in school?"

The shouting words startled Gabe, and he almost lost his footing on the rope ladder. He looked around at the sound and saw a sailor, an over-six-foot-tall giant of a man with fuzzy hair arrayed around his head like a black cloud, his beard equally fuzzy and bushy. The giant wore tar-covered trousers, a wine color peeping through, black stockings, and a yellow vest. All of it needed mending and a good wash. The giant probably needed a good wash too.

Somehow, for all the bushiness, Gabe did not feel afraid of this tall sailor. He politely said, "I have permission, sir. My father built this ship out of empty crates so I could get well."

Tucks had shouted in anger because it had been a long voyage. Long days and nights in cramped quarters, with no time to be alone, and no time to think. He had been looking forward to solitude at his favorite spot on old Gregson's Wharf. So, at first, Tucks felt anger at the boy, anger at the neat pile of crates and wood in his private place. But as Tucks observed the pale thinness of the boy and the dark circles under his eyes, his sailor heart softened toward the lad. The boy's shirt seemed meant for a larger lad, and his knee-buttoned breeches hung beneath his knees like a seaman's trousers. The wan child's unsteady gait helped Tucks accept sharing his favorite spot.

"That be all right lad. I am used to having this area to myself, but I guess I can share it with a fellow who needs to get well."

"I thank thee, sir. But I was just going home for the day. Perhaps I will see thee here again."

"Perhaps you will," Tucks answered as he watched the boy slowly limp away.

'It had been difficult to find a quiet place to observe the ships in the harbor; to watch from a distance the care and treatment of the seamen who unloaded each ship, knowing full well that the treatment shown to these laborers demonstrated the sort of Captain and officers aboard. This watchfulness had rewarded Tucks with good berths on the outbound ships and enabled him to avoid troublesome berths, at least most of the time.

'And, Gregson's Wharf was at the end of nowhere as far as shipping was concerned. Old Gregson had invested heavily in a schooner named *Polly* and vowed to await her return, although the ship had been gone for over two years. Even though his wharf stood empty, Gregson himself came to his office each day and sat smoking his great pipe, his feet up on the desk, sometimes reading a broadsheet, other times reading one of the many logbooks that stood on the shelves next to him. Since Gregson had not minded that a "mulato" seaman rested among the pilings and haphazard collection of empty crates, perhaps he did not mind the neat pile of boards and crates, and the sick child,' thought Tucks.

Crispus Attucks wondered that he cared so about children- 'Why had he stuck out his neck and taken the lashings to protect Davy? Was it because his own father had been a boy when taken from Africa, or that all his young cousins had died on the way over? Or that he, Crispus, had no wife, no children? It was all those things and yet something else. And now, he couldn't help but worry about this sick white child.

As Tucks walked home to his small cabin, in a hollow beyond the wharfs, he saw John Watson on the hill. He raised his arm in greeting, as did John.

John was grateful to see that the tall man had returned from sea. He remembered late in 1765, the first time he had seen Tucks, a tall, bushy-haired, and "black" sailor. He had wondered what a Negro was doing building a house in this part of the bay? He had felt fear as this dark stranger completed the cabin down the hill from his family. John's wife, Mary, was also unsettled about their new neighbor, but as she looked at each new person as a possible client for her laundry services, she was less worried than her husband.

John remembered the first time he had shipped out after the dark sailor's cabin was completed. He worried the entire voyage about the women alone-Mary, their three girls, his mother, and his mother-in-law. He worried even more when his ship battled a severe storm and lost a mast.

What a storm it was. At first the white-capped waves only slapped at the bobbing ship. But then the wind increased, whipping the waves into mountains that crashed over the decks. The violent wind shredded the sails, the rigging frayed and tangled, and then a monstrous wave snapped the foremast. The ship listed to one side, but once the men cut away the fore-topmast and the lines that held the bowsprit, the ship righted herself. When the storm calmed, they put in to a harbor to replace the fore-topmast. John had dreaded each moment of delay and feared what that might mean for the women at home these last six months.

When John finally returned, he saw a dark giant trudging up the hill out of the solid white of falling snow hauling something. As John grew nearer to his cabin, he was amazed at the height of the woodpile. He was equally amazed to realize the dark sailor pulled a sledge of wood toward his home.

The two men looked at each other, nodded, and silently worked together to unload the sledge. When they finished their work, the dark sailor only said, "Crispus Attucks."

The husband replied, "John Watson." As Tucks turned to leave, John remembered his manners, "I thank you." Tucks kept walking, but raised his arm in response.

John entered his home to be greeted with squeals from the girls, smiles from the mothers, and the warmth of kisses and a hug from his wife. Mary said, "He was here again, wasn't he?"

John replied, "Yes. We unloaded his sledge together. Has he been here before?"

Mary only said, "Later."

That night, after the girls were asleep in the loft, Mary, their two mothers, and John sat around the table to talk. John's mother began. "I was so afraid after you left. I did not know what to think about this new neighbor."

Mary's mother interjected, "He was so large, so tall, and he walked with a fierce stride. Just as we became used to seeing him, he was gone for a month."

Mary picked up the narrative, "Tucks, as he has asked us to call him, turned out to be a godsend. Winter began early this year, and we were getting low on wood. I used as little as I could to launder, and sent the girls out to gather what branches they could find. I even gave Hope the small hatchet to cut some thick branches."

John knew they must have been desperate for Mary to have given eight-year-old Hope the hatchet. Hope was growing up too fast as it was. She had been helping her mother with the laundry since she was six, and now six-year-old Faith was helping to care for little three-year-old Lovey. Their mothers could help by folding clothes, if they could sit while doing so, and keep an eye on Lovey for a time if she were wearing the "pudding." Even in their small cabin, Lovey could get into trouble, but with a soft bolster tied around her middle with straps holding it in place, she could fall and not hurt herself. Usually their mothers sat by the fire, keeping watch on Lovey, folding clothes or weaving the baskets in which Mary carried the clean laundry back to her customers. This relieved Faith to help Hope with the laundry.

"One evening, when the mothers and I were wondering what we would do when the wood ran out, we were frightened by a noise outside, as though something were hitting the house. We placed the heavy table in front of the door, and huddled by the fireplace. The noise stopped, and eventually we fell asleep. In the morning, the girls came in chattering about the miracle of the woodpile. I looked outside and saw our wood-pile stacked with enough cut wood to last several days. Each evening, more wood appeared, until the pile reached the size stack you see."

"We had to find out who our miracle worker was, so the mothers and I turned the lights out early one night, and waited. When we heard the wood being stacked, we lit the lamp, and walked outside in the snow to greet our savior. It was Crispus Attucks. He saw us and said, 'Better get in out of the cold.' When we tried to thank him, he responded, 'I be Tucks. You have nothing to fear from me. A seaman must help another seaman, or the ship founders. Call for me if you need anything else.' We did as he said, went back inside, and Tucks finished piling the wood. Since then, we have kept coffee warm for him, and finally convinced him to come inside for a moment to get warm before he headed home. Tucks is a good neighbor to us, John."

John thought, 'And I worried about him because he was dark skinned. I have been so very lucky! When my father died in the shipwreck off the Outer Banks, we had the room to care for Mother. When Mary's father had typhoid fever, my mother went to help Mary's mother, and stayed on with her after he died. Eventually the two mothers came to stay with us when they could no longer live on their own. I have always worried about the family when I was gone but now, maybe, I will not have to worry anymore.'

Tucks smiled as he banked his own fire and made ready for bed. 'John was home. What were those lines—something about the sailor home from the sea and the hunter home from the hill. At any rate, John was home and the women would be taken care of.' That Mary insisted on doing Tucks's laundry for free, was more payment than the bit of wood he had cut, split, carried, and piled at their cabin. But his linens were clean, and Tucks enjoyed being clean.

From now on he had an extra duty as he walked the shore. He would pick up special shells and driftwood to carve, and would share these trinkets with the little girls. 'Life is filled with miracles,' Tucks thought. 'Here I am without a wife or family, and I am given more children than I could have hoped for, and a family to replace the one I lost. I never learned what happened to my father, and my mother died the year I was pressed to sea. Now, like Job, it has all been restored.'

Tucks

After several days of cool, damp, spring-like weather, the sun shone again. At mid-morning, Gabe set out slowly for the wharf and the *Intrepid*, his ship of empty crates. He lay on the sun-warmed "deck" for a time, and then climbed to its "prow." He looked out to sea and sketched the sky and the ships in his journal. Then, on the opposing page, he made enlarged drawings of each ship, being careful to include the water line. He put down the quill and lay stretched out on the warm boards again, then looking over the side to the dock below he saw "the giant" striding toward him.

Crispus Attucks was surprised at seeing the sick child again so soon, and said, "Well, we do meet again lad. I be called Tucks. Who be you?"

Gabe could hardly believe his eyes. Tuck's hair was less bushy, slicked down, and pulled back from his face. His beard was gone, and his clothes were clean and neatly mended at the elbows. Mother, herself, could not have done better work. The giant had kind eyes, so Gabe responded, "My name is Gabriel, but folks just call me Gabe."

"Well, Gabe, it be nice to meet you again."

They sat with their backs against the tea crates that formed the *Intrepid*. Gabe told Tucks about being sick, and that his father and doctor said he needed to spend time in the sun and sea air.

Tucks said, "Well, it's true about the sun and sea air. I am always looking for the sun; the sea air comes with being on board, at least above decks. I like being up high—the higher the better. What is that book you carry about?"

"Oh, this is my journal. I write down what I see and hear each day, and sketch the ships in the harbor. Father encourages me. He gave the journal to me when I got sick. After supper each night I read to him what I have written, and then leave the book with him to look at the sketches. Sometimes in the morning I will find little notes on my sketches, or some grammar corrections. I hope to be able to go back to school in the fall, but Father said not to count on it for another year."

Crispus Attucks felt sorry for this pale boy. There was a weakness in the lad's eyes, which darted here and there, as though unable to rest. The lad's entire being said suffering. Tucks had seen boys like this on shipboard, most did not survive the voyage, and here was this strange-speaking boy trying to get well with sun and sea air. Crispus Attucks felt drawn to this lad, and the lad's need. "That must be hard, being alone here in the harbor each day. Sometimes I will come by and talk."

"It would be good to have someone to talk with," said Gabe. "I sleep in the sun and I sketch, but I get lonely too."

"This has always been my favorite spot on the wharf," said Tucks. "It be far from the noise of the busy docks, and I love the quiet. When I was your age, or even younger, I took care of cattle for a man, that be quiet time too. Later, I helped him choose cattle for breeding, and took them to market for him. When I was young, I lived like you, with my mother and father. I did not go to school, but Mother set up a school at home, and in the evenings she would teach Father and me how to read, write, and do sums. Some days she would join me when I tended cattle and show me plants that were good to eat, or good for medicine. Later on, when I was a grown man, I became a sailor, and here I am. Would you show me your journal?"

Gabe reluctantly handed it to Tucks, who leafed through the pages, looking only at the sketches. Gabe was so relieved. He did not mind Father reading his scratchings, but he did not know Tucks.

"You have done some fine sketches here. Each page seems better than the last. But you have the sails wrong on some of the ships."

"What do thee mean?"

"Well, let's look at this page. These ships with one mast are sloops. Those ships with two or three masts are schooners. The sloops and schooners are rigged for tacking, and are able to sail into the wind in coastal waters. So these ships sail between ports here at home, or to the West Indies and back. See, their sails are triangular, or cut on an angle, and set behind the mast on booms, so they can be swung from one side to the other, depending on the wind. In fact, they often sail best against the wind.

"It takes the square riggers to do well across the Atlantic. So, you want to draw the sails differently. See, the square-rigged ships have rectangular sails, set across the masts. They catch the wind on one side only. So they sail according to the Trade Winds and Prevailing Westerlys. Their sails can be taken down or put up at sea when necessary. In the stormy Atlantic, the upper rigging can be taken down to let the ship ride the waves. In the Tropics, more sail is set to catch the little breeze that there is."

"I see," Gabe said thoughtfully. "That is what Father must have meant when he said I needed to work on my attention to detail."

"Well, 'attention to detail' is what ships be all about. We spend our days onboard swabbing the decks smooth, slushing tar on the masts, coiling rope, mending the sails, restoring the rigging, and all. You never know when a storm might come up, or a privateer come over the horizon, and the ship needs to be ready to move."

"There is a lot to know to be a sailor," Gabe said with amazement.

"Well, Gabe, it depends on what kind of a seaman you want to become, an able or an ordinary seaman."

"Do not thee call thyself sailors?"

"I guess that be a general term for all who sail on ships, but it includes those on military ships too, and I do not plan to sail on any of those."

"What is it like to be a seaman?" Gabe questioned.

Seaman

"Gabe, I cannot tell you how it be for others, but I can tell you what it is like for me," Tucks began. "My first voyage be not my idea. I awoke with a headache and bad stomach in some dark, smelly place. Before I could get a sense of my situation, someone yelled, 'All hands on deck!' The ship was rocking this way and that, and the waves looked like giant monsters coming at us. Someone grabbed me and said, 'Aloft with you and lay on those yards!'

"I had no idea what he meant, but I guessed aloft meant up, though how I could climb up those rope ladders against that slanted pole waving in the storm, I did not know. I really had no time to think, but scrambled up the mast with the others and watched what they did, and then I did it too. One man fell, and I was frightened that I would fall too. I could not swim, and if I fell on the deck I would be smashed. So, I held on for dear life, and scrambled down when the others did. One of the crew, a man they called Uncle, smiled at me and said, 'Not bad for an old man and a landsman at that.' I thought, 'old man'? Uncle was twice my age.

"I discovered I was on a schooner, and the small crew be close-knit. It took a while before they accepted me—or I felt like one of them, since they be mostly lads of sixteen or eighteen, and I be already twenty-seven—an old man to them. Of course, not as old as Uncle, but too old not to know what to do. I learned fast on my first voyage, and Uncle became a good friend to me.

"Landsman, sometimes called 'common seaman,' usually be boys of various hues and some twelve to thirteen years old, at least on their first voyage. But the press gang that found me did not care what my age was. They had been hired to fill out the crew so the ship could sail."

"What is a press gang?" Gabe interrupted. "I hear Father and others talk about how terrible they are."

"Well, lad, a press gang is a group of men who go around finding seamen to fill out a crew. They do not care if the men they find belong to another crew, or just be in the streets. In my case, I was getting ready to head back to the farm, and had just stopped on my way for a bite to eat. I met these men, who seemed to be friendly, and as we walked out the door one of them hit me. I woke up in the focs'l—the place under the decks where the crew eats, sleeps, and keeps their sea chests holding all their possessions. The ship was already underway, and so I became the landsman onboard.

"My duties were endless and dirty. The parts of a ship need constant attention. First we swabbed, washing the deck and the sides of the ship. Saltwater can do a lot of damage to wood. To prevent splinters, we holystoned, or washed, the deck using a stone to sand the wood. Then we checked every rope; the mast and yardarms need to be slushed, or brushed, with tar; and the sails need constant attention. Tears and rips need mending, and weak spots reinforced before they tear. Our very lives depended on the physical condition of the ship. As we sailed further, the pumps had to be manned to empty the bilge water, and any leaks needed to be plugged. The cargo could shift in a storm, and so it needed to be checked and secured properly.

"I soon learned that as a landsman, my pay would not be much. If I wanted to earn more as an 'ordinary' or 'able' seaman, I had a lot to learn. So I set about learning how to climb the rigging in all sorts of weather, furling and unfurling sails, and knowing the different purposes and kinds of sails and lines. I learned how to use a marlinespike to restore or repair rigging with knots, splices, seizings, coverings, and turnings in. I practiced making long splices and short splices in rope, how to fit a block-strap, pass seizings to lower rigging, and a variety of knots and their purposes."

"It took many voyages and much practice, but I found the sea more to my liking than tending cattle had been. In both there be a freedom—a time alone to imagine or think. But, despite the work and almost slavery, there be a greater sense of God and the vastness of Creation at sea."

It was a perfect afternoon, the warm sun making its final appearance for the day, the water in the harbor still as glass—a moment of hesitation, a time when the whole of Creation waited for the tide to turn. Gulls were silent, standing patiently atop masts and piers, soaking in the sun, resting on one leg, looking off—somewhere. Both Gabe and Tucks stood silent too, lost in their own thoughts.

Gabe had sat through this long telling with rapt attention, even though he only half understood what Tucks had said. Gabe felt there was much to learn from Tucks, and some mysteries to solve. 'Why was his mother teaching his father to read and do sums? Why could his mother read and not his father? Where did Tucks come from? He looked dark like an African, but he had the high cheekbones of an Indian. His hair was bushy like some Africans, but he spoke well, and could read—most Africans could not. Who was the man he worked for? Did his parents work for him too? Crispus Attucks was a strange name, where did it come from? It did not sound either Indian or African. Tucks mentioned slavery at sea, what did that mean? Hard work? So much to learn.' How lucky Gabe was to have time to spend at the docks.

Tucks said, "It will be evening soon, lad, time for supper," and walked silently away.

Gabe thought, 'I have to write this all down in my journal.'

At Home

When ten-year-old Gabriel arrived home, Rafe had already cut the firewood and brought in kindling to start the stove for breakfast tomorrow. The vegetables had been gathered, water carried, and all in readiness for what lie ahead. 'Like a ship, a home is like a ship. All must be ready for what happens next. Only I am not even a landsman. I have not done anything,' Gabe thought.

Rafael said, "Hi, Gabe. Why do thee not rest before supper? Thee look a little feverish. Art thee feeling any better?"

"I am tired of being sick. I am tired of being useless. I am tired of looking feverish and needing to rest!"

Rafe quickly said, "I am sorry, I did not mean …"

"It's okay, Rafe. I am sorry too. Thee does so much and I do so little. I guess I will go sit in the window for awhile." As Gabe lay there, feeling a bit sorry for himself, he looked around at the bounty God had given him. He was alive, and that was not something the doctor had expected. He had a wonderful home and family, loving parents. His eight-year-old sister, Sarah, and his twelve-year-old brother, Rafe, were his best friends. Now, there was Tucks. 'Really,' Gabe thought as he drifted off to sleep, 'really I have a good life and should be satisfied.'

Rafe was worried about Gabe. It had been only a few weeks since Gabe had been at the wharf lying in the sun on the *Intrepid*, and, while there was some color in his cheeks today, it could be caused by fever, and his eyes were still underlined with the deepest gray. Rafe didn't want a return to the days when Gabe was truly ill, feverish, and mumbling words no one could understand, or words that made no sense. Rafe remembered, 'Father and I slept in the print shop, I ran errands and helped as I could when not in school. I remember Father and I carrying Gabriel to the kitchen and placing him in the washtub, hoping the cool water would help lower his fever. Carrying him, we realized all the sturdiness was gone from Gabe, his ribs were more visible than they had ever been. Father and I looked at each other in wonder at the lightness of Gabe's body. When the doctor came, he only shook his head. He bled Gabriel several times over the next few days. Finally Gabe's fever lessened. I shall never forget my relief when Gabe finally opened his eyes and said he was thirsty.

'I remember hearing Father talk with the doctor. The doctor said that in his experience Gabe would be bedridden for weeks after such a severe illness. And, it might take a year or more for him to return to health, if he ever did. Gabe needed rest now, and later sun and sea air to heal.

'I remember Father wondering aloud how he would keep an active young boy in bed, and not tire his already weak system. Together, he and the doctor came up with the idea of a journal. So Father took several foolscaps, folded them, and Mother sewed the pages to form a book. I cut several quills, and made sure there was ink each day. It was pure joy when Gabe began to sketch ships in the harbor. His bed had been moved close to the window in the second story above the print shop.' Coming back to the present, Rafe realized it had been two months since Gabe's illness, and Gabe's gait was still not steady. 'I hope this sea air helps,' Rafe thought.

Father came in from the print shop looking tired, but after a cup of tea, he seemed his usual cheery self. He looked at Gabe asleep on the window seat, and then at Rafe who only shrugged. Soon the aroma of onions and beans and carrots and baking bread wafted into the room, and Sarah, the youngest, came in telling them to wash up. Father gently woke Gabe, and they prepared for supper.

As they sat down to their simple meal, Rafe thought 'Gabe used to be like Sarah. He was healthy and full of spirit. Like Sarah, he could work hard, and no task was beneath him. Sarah is such a lovely little girl. She has blonde hair like Mother, and like Gabe. I might have dark hair like Father, but we all have blue eyes. I love the peacefulness of home. School is filled with talk of mobs and violence. I will be glad when the year is done and I can begin my apprenticeship. The tension is so wearing. Before Gabe was ill, our home was a sanctuary, now that peace seems threatened. Even Mother is showing the strains of it all. She rests more and smiles less, and the dark circles under her blue eyes match those of Gabe's. Gabe—I cannot imagine a world without Gabe.' Rafe shook himself mentally. 'I shall not let my worries spoil this moment.' He turned his attention to supper.

It was a healthy meal, if simple: bean and vegetable soup with a bit of salt pork for extra flavor, chunks of warm bread, cheese and apples for dessert, and lots of conversation. Father spoke of the shop and the day's news. Sam Adams was leading a crusade with businessmen to stop importing goods from England. They suggested using Colonial goods and wearing colonial homespun instead of imported fabrics. Father wondered if businesses in other areas would agree. The nonimportation of British goods would only work if most of the colonial businesses agreed.

Father's lesson for the day was how the choice of words can lead to violence, even when the essay or speaker seems to be calling for thought and reason. He reminded them of the essay in the *Boston Gazette* in October of 1765. In the essay, the writer called for his countrymen to "Awake." Not to be "cowards" or servile. They had a "Duty" as men with the "unconquerable Spirit of the ancient Britons ... the august title of Englishmen ... by the Liberty wherewith Christ have made you free" to "instruct your Representatives against promoting by and Ways of Means whatsoever, the Operation of this grievous and Burdensome law."

"Note the use of 'cowards' and 'unconquerable spirit.' These are not words that promote quiet, careful thought," said Father. "They are fighting words. And what could be meant by 'ways of means whatsoever?' They too suggest other than legal means to an end. And what were the ends used to repeal the Stamp Act?"

Rafe answered, "Colonists united."

Father said, "True, what else?"

Rafe said, "Oh, yes ... The violence against the Stamp Act Agents, the attack on Lieutenant Governor Hutchinson's home. And, more violence."

"Exactly. So, when thee speak of liberty and equality, and thee will, consider thy words carefully. It is not cowardly to refuse to be part of a mob. It is cowardly to be violent. Wars may be won with violence, but the problems that led men to that violence shall not have been solved. It is only when we look at all men, women, and children with love that those problems will be solved. We will never change the world's injustice by striking our fellow man, though we may change him by our love. We do not need to pay the tax, nor do we need to strike the man collecting it. Now ..."

The discussion turned toward Rafe and Sarah and their schools. Rafe attended the Latin School that prepared boys for Harvard. Sarah attended a private school that prepared girls to be young ladies. They both had good days, had "toed the mark," and were able to recite well.

Rafe told about one of the Martin boys, Luther, who had broken his slate on the bench when he could not get his numbers even, and how the schoolmaster had taken Luther out to "talk" with him. This new schoolmaster was different than the one before, who would have used the strap on Luther for wasting his father's money.

Father said, "Mr. Martin would not use the strap either. Luther tries hard, but might never be able to make his numbers or letters properly with his broken fingers. They healed straight after the jar fell and smashed them when he was a baby, but they shall never work as well as healthy fingers. His fingers' ability have nothing to do with his mind, which your new teacher knows quite well."

Then it was Sarah's turn. She did not say how much she wished her education were equal to that of Rafe's. She was grateful for the table talk and her time with Mother, who was teaching what her private school did not. Instead, Sarah spoke of her lessons in handwriting, and was grateful for the day's lesson in needlework. Her knitting had improved as the tension of her stitches was more even. She had even been complimented on her work by friends.

Father looked across the table and said, "Gabe, what did thee learn today?"

Gabe told them what he had learned about being a seaman, and then asked some of his questions about Tucks. Mother looked to Father, and said, "Well, son, I think those are good questions to wonder about, but I am not sure thee should ask him all the questions at once. The answers might become clear without thee asking, and thy asking would seem impertinent."

Father spoke up. "Is he the same bushy fellow thee told us about the other day?"

"Yes," said Gabe. "But today he was clean, had no beard, and his hair was tied back."

"He said he was captured by a press gang?" Father asked.

"Yes, Father, and he told me what was wrong with my sketches. I had the sails wrong on the sloops and schooners. He taught me a whole lot about being a seaman. May I continue to talk with him, Father?"

Father looked at Mother, thought for a moment, considered that Gregson would not have allowed a troublesome black man to frequent his wharf; then told his ten-year-old son, "Yes. Yes, Gabe, that will be fine. Always be sure to note in thy journal the things he says, especially about liberty. What was it he said about the sea again?"

"He said it gave him 'a greater sense of God and the vastness of Creation.'"

"He sounds like a thoughtful man. Hmm. And he can read and write, and his mother taught him. An interesting fellow," Father said. "Go to bed now, but leave thy journal with me, I want to see what he showed thee about the sails."

The children did as Father said. Gabe and Sarah went to bed and immediately fell asleep. Rafe lay awake for a while, thinking. 'I would like to meet this Tucks, and hear his adventures, that certainly would be more fun than school.' He could hear the soft sounds of his mother and father talking. The murmuring was soothing and gradually lulled him to sleep.

And Father did look. He was pleased with what he saw in the sketches and in the writing. Father still had some concerns about the sailor. He knew the stories of sailors being impressed and striking against a captain. He had heard about the lashings, mutiny, and piracy, and wondered all the more at the mention of God. 'Perhaps this Tucks had learned it from the Puritans, or the whaling Quakers. They surely had no love for customs officials or British taxation. From the first,' Father remembered, 'whaling had caused problems: from whose whale it was when it washed up on shore, to who would get the whale oil when it was caught in shoal water. When the government wanted a part of the oil, the whalers had ignored the government. As early as 1714 the Assembly listened to arguments about taxation without consent.'

Father remembered what his parents had told him about Samuel Mulford:

> An assemblyman and leader in the fight for the protection of whalers, who had even distributed his speech on this "unlawful" taxation on whale oil to others. The governor had tried to charge Mulford with libel and sedition, and expelled him from the Assembly, or legislature, but the charges were dropped when Mulford was re-elected. Mulford had sailed twice to England to protest that these customs laws "took away rights and property without consent of the governed." The laws were softened after his second voyage, as Parliament saw Mulford as a "true Englishman" fighting for his "ancient rights and liberties" against "a gang of corrupt hirelings," in this case the governor and his staff.

All this seemed a precursor of what was happening now, although Parliament did not appear to be on their side this time. Maybe it would be good to have a sailor for a friend. In fact, Father wondered if Sam Adams had learned his philosophy from Mulford. Adams had said things a little differently than Mulford when he wrote against the Stamp Act:

> The Stamp Act was made where we are in no Sense represented, therefore it was no more binding upon us than an Act which should oblige us to destroy one half of our Specie ... A Parliament of Great Britain can have no more Right to tax the colonists than a Parliament of Paris.

'That was a strong statement! Yet true,' thought Father. 'We have no representatives to speak for us in Parliament, no Sam Mulford to explain our position. And, maybe Parliament no longer sees us as true Englishmen. That indeed may be the problem. Is it possible Parliament now thinks of us as rebellious natives to be controlled rather than citizens to be represented?'

Evenings

When Father looked up from reading Gabe's journal and thinking about Parliament, Mother said, "I am worried about Gabe. While his color looks better after the time in the sun, I wonder just how safe the docks are?"

Father answered, "Rafe and I built the *Intrepid* at Gregson's out of the way of any trouble that might be brewing on the docks. I think this Tucks will be a great protection for Gabe. I like the sound of the man, although I worry about the way things are going. King George and Parliament seem to think the only way to get out of debt is to tax the colonies. If we allow their taxes, then we ultimately lose our right to tax ourselves, or govern ourselves. Our families came to the colonies to avoid tithing the Church of England, and now another tithing is upon us, taxes. Parliament's choice of taxes hits those very people who have the least ability to pay—couples getting married, a man needing a license to start a business, and others like us who print pamphlets, newspapers, bills, or legal documents.

"Thankfully, the Stamp Act was repealed, but in return Parliament declared that the British government has total power to legislate any laws governing the colonies 'in all cases whatsoever.' King George seems to respond only when the colonists cause trouble, to respond only to violence, and that is not ever good. Violence begets violence. The winter was quiet, but I worry what the summer will bring. This Tucks might be a very good thing for us all. But I will ask around to see what anyone knows about him."

Mother responded, "Please do. It seems the whole town thinks violence is the answer to any issue, and I do not want Gabe or Rafe caught in the middle."

"Nor do I," Father responded. "But I like that Gabriel is interested in someone and something at last. I remember his illness. I have felt some guilt going to the Yearly Meeting, leaving you with Gabe, ill with a cold, and only Sarah to help. When Rafe and I returned home, excited about the presentation of John Woolman, we discovered a severely ill Gabe. He lay there feverish, sometimes mumbling words we could not understand, or words that made no sense, and you, my dear Charity, were so pale, so tired. Your sister, Martha, came and stayed forever it seemed, though in reality only four weeks. Eight-year-old Sarah was sent to Martha's and the oldest cousin, Meg, took care of her. Rafe and I slept on pallets in the print shop while Martha slept in the boys' room or in the sitting room.

"The doctor thought Gabe might be contagious, but luckily no one else became ill, except you my dear, who spent more time in bed than you were out of it. You were so worried about Gabe that you took shifts with Martha the first few weeks. One of you watched at Gabe's bedside day and night; you only rested when Martha insisted. When you became pale and lost weight, Aunt Martha refused to let Sarah come home until you were yourself again.

"I remember Martha as a happy person with a merry song on her lips, though she sang loud and off-key A tall, bony woman and thin as a rail, she tied back her bright-red hair with a ribbon, or sometimes in a black net."

"Yes, dear," Charity said. "And she had two dresses, one for meetings and one for everyday. The meeting dress was black, but the daily dress was green-dyed homespun."

Father added, "I felt bad that eleven-year-old Rafe disliked Martha at first. He did not understand why she had to come and Sarah had to go, though he felt important sleeping in the same room with his father. We had lots of quiet talks about John Woolman, and what it means to be a Quaker. I missed all that special time with Rafe after Martha left for home, but I was happy to have our family reunited, and Gabe getting better."

Mother added, "I was always sorry that Martha died in childbirth a few months later, so Gabe never really got to know her. His Uncle Albert remarried soon after and moved west to the mountains. You said he needed a wife to care for the five children, the oldest fifteen, and the youngest four. And, he could not stand to live in 'Martha's house,' as he always called their home." Thinking out loud, Charity said softly, "I too am happy to see Gabe with an interest in life again, for a time I wasn't sure if anything would interest him again."

What Gabe and Rafe did not know was that their father, Matthew Bellson, an independent printer, sometimes met with Sam Adams and James Otis in the evenings. Matthew was not known for having any ties with the Sons of Liberty, so it seemed only natural that Adams and Otis would stop by nightly with reports and speeches that needed printing. Bellson also printed reports and notices for Lieutenant Governor Hutchinson, and sometimes Governor Bernard. As other printers, Bellson accepted material on both sides of any issue to stimulate readership, and provide forums for public discussion. Besides, most essayists and letter writers did not sign their names but chose an alias that best suited their position on an issue. Thus, Adams or Otis might leave the print shop as a representative from Hutchinson or Bernard arrived.

If someone wanted work printed first thing in the morning, they would drop off the work the night before. It took time to set the lead type for the press, letter by letter, so any headstart with material was helpful. Bellson's print shop was small and took any size project, usually simpler work the larger presses would find inconvenient. Sometimes Charity would help Father in the evenings to get ready for the next day, as she had when they first took over the print shop from Matthew's father.

They often sat up late in the small living room off the print shop. It was a convenient spot. During the day there was a sunny window seat, where Gabe could rest, and through a doorway was the kitchen. A stove jutted into this small sitting room through the kitchen's wide open hearth, and kept both rooms warm. This little room was a good place for Mother and Father to talk privately, as their own bedroom was above this sitting room, while the boys' room was above the print shop, and Sarah's room above the kitchen. Sound carried in their little home, so privacy was cherished.

Mother and Father knew that Rafe would be joining Father in the print shop when the school year ended. School had not been the fit for Rafe that it was for Gabe, and Rafe was itching to get started in some apprenticeship, especially if he could stay home.

Many boys had to quit school to become apprenticed, and leave their homes to live with their new master. An apprentice was like an indentured servant in that he lived with the family teaching him, and was bound to them for seven years, twenty-four hours a day, seven days a week. He could not leave their shop or home without permission. But, in return for his servitude, the young man learned a trade.

Matthew's apprentice, Charles Cotter, was lucky. Since his mother lived next door to the print shop, Charles was permitted to return home after work and could continue to care for his mother. Lucky also for Rafe, who wanted to quit school, as he would be able to stay home joining Father in the print shop. Lucky for Father, also, that Charles, in thankfulness for the years of freedom, was staying another year beyond his time, so Rafe could be trained.

This evening, Father and Mother quizzed Adams and Otis about Tucks. Sam Adams said he was sure he had met him the year before after a talk with a group of sailors. Adams had thought Tucks was probably a runaway slave, though the press gang story explained a lot. Although Adams found Tucks to be articulate, he fit the description of a runaway slave Adams had read about several years ago.

The master, a Mr. Brown, had advertised for a runaway, described as "a mulatto about twenty-seven, named Crispus, six feet and two inches tall." Mr. Brown had offered "ten pounds old tenor" reward, as well as "all expenses." From what little Adams had been able to discover, Crispus Attucks's mother had been an Indian, and his father a slave. They had lived on a farm outside of Boston, although they had made many trips into town for their master. There had been no sign that Tucks would have run away on his own. But, being free now, there was no reason he would return to his old master.

Otis suggested that this friendship could be good for the cause. Since Tucks could read and write, he would be of use to the other sailors and be able to share what they were thinking.

Adams and Father agreed. Mother still wondered about Gabe spending time with Tucks. She had heard too many tales about rowdy, drunken sailors with their foul language, although so far there had been no sign of either with Tucks. She reluctantly agreed, but said, "If there is the slightest danger to Gabe he comes back from the docks, despite his newfound interest, despite his need for sun and sea air."

Father agreed, and said he would have Gabe share some of his journal at supper each night, and then Father would read it carefully in the evening to check for any possible problems.

Worthless and Crazy

There was a knock at the print shop door. Adams and Otis left, glaring at the representative from Hutchinson, who had entered with Governor Bernard's printing request.

Hutchinson's representative glared back, then said to Father, "Well, Bellson, I do not know how you stand 'worthless' and 'old crazy' there." Before Father could respond, the representative continued, "I know, I know. A small print shop has to take in every order that comes to it, and the people have a right to both sides. Well, if those two have their way, Hutchinson's Albany Plan will be fulfilled. Oh, I know, many want Ben Franklin's plan—cooked up with radicals—colonies with their own government and represented in Parliament. But Hutchinson's idea of stronger British control makes the most sense. If there had been British soldiers instead of colonial militia in charge, the violence to Hutchinson's home would not have been tolerated. If we are English colonies, then we ought to be ruled by the English, not a colonial mob." He paused for breath. "Okay, Bellson. Here is the print order. Hutchinson probably would not use you if you were not on my way home." With that he left.

Father closed the door and sighed in relief. 'Worthless'? 'Crazy'? 'If Hutchinson felt this way, no wonder things were in a mess. Did Governor Bernard feel this way too? The Governor had always been a supporter of the colony. While it was true that Adams might be short of cash, and Otis might have moments of instability, worthless and crazy they were not. In fact, they were the leading opponents of Governor Bernard and Lieutenant Governor Hutchinson.' Matthew sighed again as he looked at the proclamations he was to print the next day. After closing the shutters and locking the door to the print shop, Father entered the small sitting room.

Matthew joined Charity in front of the stove. It was a peaceful room, if sparsely furnished. Charity sat in a comfortable chair upholstered in a cabbage rose pattern, a wedding gift from her relatives in England. Matthew's chair was simple, but the padded back and seat matched the green in Charity's chair. Charity's oval rag rug softened the wide floor boards in front of the stove, on either side of which were bookcases with shells and a few books. The small table beside Matthew's chair held an oil lamp and a Bible. Another lamp was lit on the bookcase closest to Charity's chair, lighting the yarn as she knit and capturing her hair in a halo of light. Across from the stove, the window seat had been painted a light green, as had the walls above the white wainscot that flowed around the room. A pale green, hand-knit comforter lay folded on the seat next to two quilted pillows. The simple cream-colored homespun curtains on the windows above the window seat were closed against the night. In a far corner stood a spinning wheel, with room for a loom in the winter.

The door to the print shop now closed, Matthew put his hand on Charity's shoulder and kissed her forehead as he passed through to the kitchen. He locked that door, put another log in the kitchen hearth, as the spring nights were still cold, then joined Mother before the warm stove.

As Matthew sat down, he sighed, "Worthless and crazy."

"Worthless and crazy?"

"Yes, dear. That's what Hutchinson's man called Adams and Otis."

"Neither is worthless or crazy, though I suppose those who oppose them may think so." Charity added candidly, "I suppose if you aren't rich, or interested in making money, like Sam Adams, then some might think you are worthless. In fact, if he had not remarried as he did, his lack of support for his children might make him seem worthless. Luckily he has a wife who knows how to manage money and a household. Sam also projects a deceptive presence, a bit portly with a sallow complexion, a twitching mouth and a sunken chest. His dark blue eyes show intelligence if one looks closely, but at first glance seem weak against his prominent nose and high forehead. His outside belies the man inside."

"You are correct, my dear. I only admire his mind, ignore the physical, and forget the practical side of things. Adams is working so hard to protect us from those who would control us, he forgets the daily necessity of food and clothing for children."

Charity said lovingly, "But you never forget your wife or children or our needs. You are a good husband and good provider, Matthew. I do worry about James Otis, though. I believe his mind is going. He often has trouble keeping track of a simple conversation, though I hear he follows those legislative arguments with clarity."

Matthew looked at his lovely, intelligent wife. Her light brown hair had a few strands of gray in it. 'When had that happened?' he wondered. 'Gabe's illness and her own had taken much from her. She wore his favorite pale-yellow dress, now faded from many washings, that hung loosely on her. When had she lost the weight? All the sickness, all the politics, he really needed to take better care of her.'

"Let's head upstairs, my dearest. There is nothing we need to start on tonight, and we both need a peaceful rest," Matthew said, looking lovingly at Charity.

"Yes, dear. We do need some peaceful rest."

As they lay down to sleep, Matthew's mind was on Charity and the need to protect his family. Charity thought of all that had happened this long day: Gabe and Tucks; taxation; worthless and crazy; Rafe leaving school soon; and Sarah, Sarah who had seen so much in her young life. But grace came down on them both, their worries departed, and they slept peacefully in each other's arms.

There was no peace in the heart of James Otis. As he and Sam Adams left the print shop, Adams could see that Otis was working himself into a nervous frenzy, so he began to remark on their fortunate choice in printers, and the good work they had done that day. Otis kept looking back at the print shop and muttering 'crazy and worthless' under his breath. They had listened at the door of the print shop hoping to learn what the government planned. Instead, they had heard the insults.

Adams changed the topic to Crispus Attucks. Otis ceased his muttering and repeated what he had said to the Bellsons. "I believe this sailor may be of great use to us. If young Gabe is as bright as I think he is, then the journal he writes will be invaluable in granting us awareness of the thoughts of the dock workers."

Adams agreed, then asked, "Are you sure the docks will be a safe place for the lad?"

Otis thought a moment, and then said, "Yes. Gregson's Wharf is safe, and I believe the journal will tell us if things are not. Gabe is just a lad, an ill one at that, so he is a threat to no one. The key will be the character of this Tucks. Will he be safe for the boy?"

"Let us hope so." As Otis took a look back at the print shop, Adams continued, "Now, what shall we discuss with the Sons of Liberty tonight?"

"Mobs," Otis said.

"Mobs?"

"Yes. I think it's time to discuss the destruction of the Oliver and Hutchinson homes. If we are to continue to make progress with the other colonies, we cannot be seen as unruly radicals, but instead as thoughtful, protesting, citizens."

"You are right as usual, Otis," Sam Adams said. "But even with Ebenezer MacIntosh in jail, there will still be riots. The people, merchants as well as laborers, have taken about all they can. They see the poor. They see the Olivers and Hutchinsons driving around in their carriages and know that for every wealthy man there are ten who are not. They also know what the rich crowd believes about the ordinary person. Didn't they try to get rid of town meetings? Didn't they support the Currency Act that banned paper money? Didn't they hear Hutchison and his friends refer to the impoverished as 'rabble' and the caucus as a 'herd of fools, tools, and sycophants'?'

Otis replied, "Yes, and they heard those same politicians say that 'poverty was the best inducement for industry and frugality' and that 'the common people of this town and country lived too well.' I told them they did not live half well enough. But that utter, mindless destruction can't be repeated."

"It was one thing to hang Oliver in effigy for agreeing to be a stamp commissioner. It was quite another to go to Hutchinson's house and break mirrors and windows, demolish the furniture, and tear up his gardens. They broke in at dinner, using axes against the doors, then chopped up the furniture, and smashed through walls until the house was an empty shell. They not only dug up the gardens, but scattered books and papers, and then stole anything of value. I pitied Hutchinson. But I was most angry at the theft. Ebenezer MacIntosh, who orchestrated this, has much to answer for. I am glad he is in jail. We won't write a word to help him. This wasn't an angry mob dissuading a stamp commissioner, these were vandals—destructive thieves—and it will not happen again."

Adams had listened to Otis speak about the destruction before, and he and others had been appalled at the mob's actions. Yet Adams knew, what Hutchinson would never understand, 'the people were angry, furious at the display of wealth in the midst of poverty.' They had heard Hutchinson and others of his crowd disparage those who suffered economic hardship, all the while fattening their purses. And where had those economic hardships come from? The same England, the same Parliament that said America had to pay for the war, but could not cross the mountains now that the war had been won. The same voices that said the colonies could be sources of raw materials and purchasers of finished products, but could not be producers of finished goods.

Adams said, "So, what do we tell the Liberty boys? They have been educated in our schools and can read the papers. They are aware of what is happening and who is in control of the happenings. We know that Liberty depends on the education of its people for its protection. We also know Hutchinson and others believe that education of the average person is 'a needless expense, and imposition upon the rich in favor of the poor.' If Hutchinson and his crowd have their way, we won't have an educational system. People are so much easier to control if they can't debate the issues."

"Yes, yes, but now that MacIntosh is out of the picture, we need reasonable leaders who won't let events get out of hand. We need to explain that the destruction gained us nothing except the resignation of James Oliver as stamp commissioner. It only solidified the opinion of Thomas Hutchinson that the working class is rabble."

"You are right, of course. So, tonight the subject is mobs!" replied Adams, grateful that Otis was thinking clearly now.

A Peculiar People

The next warm afternoon, Tucks again joined Gabe at the *Intrepid* and asked for a tour of the ship Father and Rafe had made for Gabe. Gabe rattled on about the deck and the prow, and how far he could see beyond the harbor. The prow was elevated—one stack of crates higher than the main deck.

Tucks said, "Well, this be a mighty sturdy ship. What do you call her?"

Gabe responded, "The *Intrepid*."

"*Intrepid*. A mighty fine name. It means being brave and adventurous when others think you are foolish ... Sometimes one has to act, even if one would rather not, even if one is afraid. There be things worth fighting for, like freedom." Tucks sat thoughtfully for a while, observing the *Intrepid*. Then he asked, "What are these two openings?"

"They are the impressment decks and the slave hold."

"You going to impress some sailors and do some slave trading are you?"

"No, of course not," Gabe said quickly. "My father and brother built these so my brother and I could have a small taste of what these conditions could be like. My brother, Rafe, and my father went to a Yearly Meeting of the Quakers and heard a speaker explain how horrible slavery was. After the business part of the meeting, they heard the speaker, John Woolman, discuss the horrors of slavery, quoting often from the writings of Anthony Benezet. I remember the words Rafe repeated to me:

... should we consider ourselves only spectators, when the cruel catch innocent children employed in the fields, when we hear their cries of fear at being captured, or should we think about it happening to our own families, having our own children carried off by savages; we have to admit that such proceedings are contrary to the nature of Christianity. Just imagine, neighbors capturing children in the fields to sell to others who bring them to America for slaves. Those 'others' claim to be Christian, yet profit from the enslavement of those men, women, and children.

"He spoke of the men, women, and children brought from Africa, stowed like cordwood so captains could bring as much 'black gold' to the colonies as their ships could hold. I tried hard, but I could not imagine what that might be like to be stacked like cordwood, on shelves, no place to move, chained, and having to lie in filth. Rafe said he could not imagine what it would be like to come over in a slave ship, so Father had us lie for two hours in the slave hold so we could imagine it."

"Both of you lay in there? It be hardly big enough for one of you!"

"Father said that is how he imagined the journey. Our two hours seemed like forever. Rafe needed to relieve himself, but we had been asked not to move, so we began to imagine what being a slave transported over the sea might have been like.

"Rafe told me John Woolman spoke of fairness and liberty, two concepts to be thought about. Woolman said: 'to live in ease and plenty by the toil of those who violence and cruelty have put in our power is neither consistent with Christianity nor common justice.' In fact, he said, 'Where slave-keeping prevails, pure religion and sobriety declines.' After all, this 'clearly contradicts Christ's command that we love one another ...' But the meaning was clear to me, and to Father, not that we ever had a slave to free.

"John Woolman had seen slavery at its worst. He had seen the cruelty of some owners. He had seen the slave auctions, and he had seen the depravity on the large plantations: the children of slave and owner, and the pain in a wife's eyes as she attempted to ignore the reality of these children. Woolman had spoken gently to all, but learned to avoid some plantations as he made multiple journeys to the area. His speech was often impassioned, but never accusatory, and when he found himself needing to speak more plainly, he took the guilty person aside.

"Rafe said Woolman spoke about the condition of slavery itself. On large plantations, and even here in New England, Africans could be bought and sold like cattle, with someone checking their limbs and teeth as they might a horse. He talked about the separation of families:

children torn from their mothers and sold to one owner, the father to another, and the wife/mother to yet another. He said all men deserved better than that. Rafe said all Quakers should set their slaves free. Woolman's words made a powerful impact on Rafael, who needed to share his newfound beliefs with anyone who would listen, and I was a willing listener."

"Why would your father care about slaves?"

"We are Quakers and we do not believe in violence. Truth, sincerity, and simplicity rule our lives. We also believe that possessions do not lead to inner peace or joy."

"What kind of religion be that?"

"We are Christians who call each other Friends. We believe in human goodness, because God is in us all. There is human evil, but we must try to get rid of it. According to Father, we Friends have been against slavery and the ill treatment of slaves for a long time," explained Gabe.

"You folks must be a peculiar kind of people."

"I guess we are. I know there aren't many of us here in Boston, or in Massachusetts. Most of our people were driven out of the colony as soon as they arrived. Some, like Mary Fisher and Ann Austin, had their books burned and were sent to Barbados. Four others were hanged right here on Boston Common. We were thought to be heretics or practitioners of witchcraft, so Quakers were not welcome in a Puritan Massachusetts. We believe that God is in everyone, and speaks to each one of us. His presence is truly a guiding spirit in our lives. We do not have churches or ministers; we do not take oaths; we do not tithe to the Church of England, and we do not believe in war or violence as the answer to anything."

"So, some Friends own slaves?" Tucks asked.

Gabe responded quietly, with feeling. "Some still do, but Friends are slowly freeing their slaves. Friends are being sure freedom does not mean poverty, and so are paying their slaves for the years they worked. Their former masters are hiring some of the freed slaves, others set up their own businesses. Friends have set up schools for the children and for adults of slaves, ex-slaves, and Indians who have not been taught to read. We hope soon there will be no more slaves owned by Friends!" Gabe said passionately.

"You really be a peculiar people. I hope the day comes when there will be no more slaves." After a long pause, Tucks added, "My father be a slave."

The Prince

"I be a slave too, for a while," said Crispus Attucks. "My father used to tell me about his life in Africa. He was a prince there. Even so, he had work to do; he watched the cattle for his village. In his village, cattle were the symbol of a man's wealth, and the wealth of the village. So, cattle watching be an important work. In drought times, hyenas or lions would come in packs to attack the calves, sometimes they would even take down a full grown bull."

Gabe sat listening, raptly. "What could your father do, if they came for the cattle?"

"Well, my father was not alone, his cousins and brothers were there too. His work was to keep a lookout. The boys had only a spear each for defense, but the best defense was to herd the cattle together in a safer location. My father had great eyesight then, and could see a far distance. When he be young, the best protection was not to go too far from where the men hunted, so they could be called for help. As they grew older, he and his cousins became proficient with spears and less in need of help when danger threatened. Most of the time, there was no danger, but in severe drought, despite their skill, the boys often lost a few cattle. My father would tell me his adventures. Sometimes there would be snakes sunning themselves on the rocks, he would stay a distance away but keep an eye on them all the time.

"Once, when I was about twelve, my father took me to a large hill. We could see the ocean in one direction and forests in other directions. He took me by the shoulders and said, 'There be many choices.' Facing me toward the west, he told me, 'There be the West, a land unexplored, a land of trees and animals, mountains and maybe even deserts. We do not know how far it goes, maybe to another ocean. This offers unlimited ways to discover.' Facing me toward the east, he told me, 'There be the ocean; there somewhere is Africa, and my village, and your aunts and uncles. There also be work, storms, and unimagined sights.' Facing me north, he said, 'There be your mother's people. They read and write and speak English and their own language. Half of you belongs to them, as half of you belongs to Africa. I do not know what lies ahead for her people, but their history with the white man has been as severe as mine.' Lastly, he faced me south. 'There lies Boston, a great city, but a city of pain for dark-skinned ones such as us. There you will be feared for the color of your skin, envied because you read and write, ignored because you have no money. But there is honest work in Boston, should you choose that direction.' He reminded me that Natives had few choices. Slaves had fewer choices. But I was neither, and both, so I had many choices."

Crispus continued, "When I be a boy and tending cattle, I used to pretend on some days that I was in Africa, and looking out for lions or hyenas. The pasture became grasslands; the forest edging the pasture became jungle. There be snakes to look out for here, too, as well as wolves and panthers. Like my father, I too had to look out for danger, but unlike my father, I had a barn close by where the cattle would be safe.

"I liked my father's stories of Africa, but after a while I quit asking for them, for as I grew older Father grew more sad when he told them."

As Tucks paused, Gabe interjected, "Would thee tell me some of the stories?"

"Well, some of my favorite stories be those the traders told when they visited his village. In the first story, the traders would tell about their adventures across the sea of sand. They said it took weeks to cross this land-sea, and if they had not known where to find water, they all would have perished. The traders used camels, beasts that could carry heavy loads and people across this sand-sea. These beasts had wide feet so they did not sink in the sand, and they had huge humps on their backs where they stored water.

"No, Gabe, the traders could not drink that water," Tucks said to

Gabe's questioning look. "No, this water was stored, somehow, so the camels could use it as they needed it, and this let the camels go for days without a new water supply."

Tucks continued, "The traders told of their experience with a sandstorm. I guess you can see these storms coming a far distance away, and luckily there be some caves nearby. They were able to get the camels and themselves in one of the caves just as the storm hit. The cave was deep, so they moved away from the entrance, where sand was already piling up. When they lit a fire, they were amazed to see the cave walls painted with figures of men hunting, growing crops, and even swimming. The traders said they had heard a traveler say that he had proof the sea of sand was once a sea of water, but everyone just laughed at him. Now the traders said they wondered if the traveler be telling the truth.

"They also told about a wonderful city called Timbuktu. From what they said it must have been great. They said it used to be a major city where wise men from all over the world would come to read and to talk with other wise men. They said not much be left of the city now, but people who still lived there would tell the stories of the wise men."

"Tell me more," Gabe said, awestruck.

"Another story they told was of something called the gold/salt trade. According to the traders, these happened years ago in a place called Mali. Traders would come and leave a pile of salt at a certain spot. Then they would go away a distance. Other traders would see the salt, and leave gold. Then they too would go away a distance. The first set of traders would look at the gold, and if it were enough, they would take the gold and leave. If it was not enough, they would just go away a distance. The second set of traders would add additional gold, then they would go away a distance. When the first traders were pleased, they would take the gold and leave. Then the second traders would take the salt and go on their way. In this way, the two sets of traders never saw each other, and no arguments happened."

"What if one of the sides did not get as much as they wanted?"

"Well, Gabe, then they would simply take the gold or salt away. They would check back once in a while to see if the other side had changed its mind, otherwise they would go to the next trading site."

"Imagine trusting each other in that way!"

"Yes. I cannot imagine that sort of trade happening today."

"Do thee have any other stories?" Gabe asked eagerly.

Crispus Attucks paused, deciding whether or not to tell this next story to this weak child. "This story is about my father. It is not a happy story," he said as he looked at Gabe intently. Seeing the honesty and sincerity in this "peculiar" child's tired eyes, and feeling the need to tell someone, he said, "I remember the last evening, after my father finished telling about the circle in his village, how they all used to sit around a fire in the evenings and retell stories of hunts, when he said:

It's time you understood the whole story. My aunts and uncles and cousins all lived in the same village. Days we followed the cattle, our wealth, but we also swam on hot days, or pretended to be lions or monkeys. We ran and laughed; we learned to make spears and throw them. Life was golden like the African sun.

Then they came. These pale-faced humans with their guns and chains. My cousins and I were caught. Metal circles were put on our ankles and chains were attached through rings until all of us were connected. When one put his right foot forward, we all did. If one man stumbled, we held him up, for if he fell we would also. We marched for days across grassland and through jungle with short stops for water and a little bread. A few tried to fight back and were whipped. A couple of boys refused to eat and died one night, one of them was my youngest cousin. These boys were unchained from us and left lying there for the animals. I could not give my cousin a proper burial.

We finally reached the sea. Huge waves came crashing in. I had seen the sea before, but never like this. The wind tore through palms and the water frothed, then the downpour. It was as though the very gods did not want us to set sail.

We shivered in our chains as we waited, for what we did not know. If we had, we would have found a way to die there too, as others had. When the storm eased we were rowed out to a huge boat. I had seen the small boats of fishermen, but nothing like this one with tall masts and lines and canvas. When we arrived on deck, we were given a thin soup, while the smaller boats went to shore for the others. Before the next boats arrived we were taken below ... to hell.

Many were already there, lying on planks, on shelves. Each man lay close to the other. There was no room to roll over, or sit up, or change position in any way. As each row filled, our feet were chained again. I was separated from my cousins, and I already felt the fear in all of us. The moaning and crying for deliverance was painful to hear. There we were, waiting until the cargo, the other Africans, were loaded. The ship was already rocking in the water, and when the ship finally began to move, many became sea sick. You can only imagine the smell of all those bodies, and no way to relieve yourself, except where you lay.

Storms made it even worse—the rolling, the fear—would we sink? Many

could not survive the fear and died. Once in a great while, I do not know how often, we would be brought up in groups on deck. They would pour water over us to clean us, and some poor soul would scrub and clean where we had lain. The fresh salt air gave me strength, but no hope of freedom for land was nowhere to be seen. When the women were brought on deck, we men listened to their screams. We could only imagine what might be happening. Each morning we listened, counting the splashes to see how many had died in the night, usually four or five. I heard one of the crew say we slaves were the stronger, only one third of us died, while almost half the crew would die of accidents or disease on the voyage.

When we finally arrived in Boston, we were taken into a large stone build-
ing with a dirt floor. I looked around for my cousins, but discovered that none
of them had survived. In groups, we were inspected, washed down, and given
a clean cloth over our privates. Then we stood on a platform and people bid
on us. Some looked in our mouths, or at our privates, to see how young or
how strong we were. I was a young man, only twelve, about your age, when
our owner bought me. Every day I know, if either you or I do not please our
master, our owner, he can do what he wants with us. Even kill us. In Africa I
was prince, the younger prince. Here I am nothing."

Tucks had to pause before continuing. This next part was as difficult
to tell as his father's passage to America. This wasn't just his father's story
though; this was Tuck's story, his life's sadness. Gabe sat silently, knowing something even more awful was to come.

Crispus Attucks took a deep breath, squared himself and began
again. "Then my father became silent. Gradually a look of anger, bitterness, and hatred came over his face. I had seen him cry on some occasions,
saying, 'I am nothing here. In Africa, I was a prince!' Usually my mother
and I would hug him, telling him we loved him and needed him. That
he was something!

"But this evening, he pushed us away. The silence in the cabin grew
thick, dark, black. I could taste, feel, the black thickness. There was no
warmth or light from the fire that could penetrate this thick black fog.
My father got up from his chair and walked out the door, away from slavery, away from us, away from his nothingness. I never saw him again."

Gabe sat for a moment; he could not imagine a life without his own
father. He could not think of what to say. 'How terrible' seemed an
empty thing to say. Finally he asked the question on his mind, "Were
thee frightened?"

"Yes. My mother and I did not know what to think when he walked
out. He had never looked that way before, not even when he told us
about being captured as he walked the path to get water. Not even when
he spoke of the chains, or the sight of the ships, or the passage to the colonies. So we did not know what to think. We just kept waiting for him to
come back inside the cabin.

"My mother finally sent me to my pallet in front of the fire. She must
have sat up all night, for I awoke to see her sitting in the chair by the
table, asleep. That day we went about our usual chores, and I completed
most of my father's chores. For several days, I do not know how long, we
thought he would come back. But he never did."

Gabe asked, "Did thee ever hear what happened to him?"

"No, I never did. Mr. Brown was kind, but I was the son of a slave and thus a slave, though my mother had never been a slave. He gave me much freedom but not the 'un-owned' kind. After that, my mother and I could spend more free time with her people, but by the time I be a man, I realized I did not fit there."

"Who were thy mother's people?" Gabe asked, the question slipping out before he caught himself.

"That be a story for another day," Tucks said, and rose looking seaward. Man and boy watched the harbor, and beyond it the sea. The sky clouded over, the water in the harbor darkened. Both thought of their fathers.

Gabe asked, "Did the slaves ever rebel?"

"I have heard of some who did, on the *Eagle Sally*, the *Elizabeth and Henry*, and the *Ferral Galley*. But my father never spoke of any. I would think it a difficult thing to attempt, especially with no land in sight. I cannot imagine that the slaves would be able to navigate the ship, and it would be a special case if the mates would navigate for them." Crispus Attucks paused. "Lad, you have listened well. I should not have burdened you with my stories. It will be evening soon, time for supper." After a moment of silence, Tucks walked thoughtfully away.

Gabe wanted to say thank you for the stories, even the sad ones, but Tucks did not want to hear from Gabe. He needed to walk away, and Gabe let him.

Gabe thought about what Tucks had said. It answered some of the questions he had, but raised others. 'Does my father know about the capture and chains and the passage of slaves?' But the hardest question was one he asked himself. 'What would I do, or feel or think if my father left, and I never heard from him or about him again? To lose a father!'

Inner Light

When ten-year-old Gabriel arrived home that evening, he was more tired and agitated than usual. During the long, slow walk from the wharf, his mind replayed the horror of the slaves' passage, and the strange departure of Tucks's father. He went to his window seat, buried himself under the comforter, and quickly fell into a troubled sleep with dreams of capture and chains. When he awoke, Gabe could hardly wait for Father to come home so they could talk.

When his father came into the room, Gabe said urgently, "Father, thee must tell me more about John Woolman and what he said about slavery. It is terrible … horrible … cruel."

Seeing Gabe unusually agitated and about to work himself into a fever, Father said calmly, "What has upset thee so?"

"Tucks told me he lost his father, who was captured, and went to hell and …"

"Whoa, settle down. Come here." Father put his hand on Gabe's forehead. "Thee art feverish, Gabe. Thee needs to calm thyself. I promise you, we will have supper and talk, and spend as much time together as thee needs."

Gabe nodded. His father's quiet voice and promise helped Gabe to calm.

Conversation at supper followed the usual pattern: events of the day and a lesson about language, this time about a couplet in the *Gazette* last year:

> To make us all Slaves, now you have lost Sir! The Hope,
> You have but to go hang yourself. —We'll find the Rope."

Gabe thought to himself, 'Yes, we will hang all the slavers!' then realized the evil in this thought. 'How can I ever look at a man or a Friend who owns slaves again without anger?'

Father explained, "This is another example of words calling for violence, when they seem not to. They seem to say, if it is wrong to make us slaves, then slavery of our fellow creature is wrong. But that is not the point being made. The speaker is really saying, people should hang the man who would make us a slave. Even though the message seems to say, go hang yourself, the unspoken message is we'll hang you. Always think carefully about how words that may seem innocent are really a hidden call for violence."

When the family gathered again after the supper chores were done, Rafe, Gabe, Sara, and Mother listened carefully as Father shared what he knew of John Woolman and others. "John Woolman is guided by an inner light, a special understanding of what is true and what is not true. He is a mystic who has a special gift of sharing his light with others. As early as the age of twenty-three, the Monthly Meeting in Burlington named him a minister, one of the youngest to be so recorded by Friends," Father began.

"John Woolman maintains that the principles of Christianity demand that no one should be a slave. If the Golden Rule was always followed, there would be no slavery. While he was passionately against slavery, John worked through love with those who owned slaves; and his quiet, kindly persuasion changed many minds.

"John is not the only Friend to feel this way about slavery, there were many before him. For example, Thomas Hazard, called 'College Tom,' refused to take his father's slaves, and ran his farm with hired labor. He convinced other friends of his to free their slaves too. And in Rhode Island, freed slaves were given a security of one hundred pounds, so they would not become a public charge. Also, Bishop Berkley, who felt slaves were fellow human beings and urged that slaves be baptized, said slaves should be looked on as men and women who have the same bodies, the same souls as any other human. They can be taught, they can reason, and they can be saved.

"Anthony Benezet followed this philosophy and taught reading, writing, and Christianity to both Africans and Indians. He said that in his teaching, he found Negroes had the same ability to learn as whites, and the same talents. He also was friends with John Woolman and published many of his articles. Benezet sent copies of them to Quarterly and Yearly Friends' meetings in all the colonies. Richard Smith, of Groton,

Connecticut, freed his slave saying the Lord had given him the insight to see the cruelty of slavery.

"The colony of Pennsylvania banned the import of slaves as early as 1712. The southern colonies were less interested, though they should have been for they had slave uprisings as early as 1739. Yearly meetings in Virginia warned members against slave trading as early as 1722, and in 1740 warned that Quakers should not serve on the patrols to keep slaves from running away. Friends should have seen that their treatment of these Africans must be wrong if their slaves felt violence the only way to freedom.

"In fact, it was on a journey to Virginia that made John Woolman realize the evil of slavery, not just because of the cruelty to these humans, but because of the danger it brought to those who owned them. He saw the increase of vice and corruption that traffic in human beings brought to those involved. It was as if a black cloud of sin hung over the southern colonies, and he feared the future damage such sin would do to those colonies.

"Woolman hated slavery. He told the Society of Friends that Christian brotherhood applied equally to all men, as all men in all nations were the children of the same Father, and that the same Shepherd looks after all, both black and white. All men are entitled to the same freedom, the same search for happiness and the Light of God. Slavery removes the freedom and search for God from the minds of both the owners and the slaves. Both live lives of anxiety, which limits freedom and inhibits the search for God.

"John is true to his beliefs that acquiring money is unimportant and that war is wrong. He worked to remind Friends of their belief in peace and that slavery was the worst of evils for it contaminated society at every level. What a great man he is!"

"Father," Gabe said, much calmer now. "How can thee know all this?"

"Gabe, I read and listen. Education is so important, and to deny it to any of our fellow creatures is to deny them the ability to think and make the right choices. As the revelation of George Keith stated, 'God placed the divine light in all of us; we all hold something of God within ourselves. This Light reminds us to avoid sin; it leads us to the Truth.' But we men are weak, and ignore the Light within. Tucks has shared a powerful witness to thee. Thee have been blessed with a truth, a reality of life few white men have. I have a feeling he has much more to share. I too long for a time without slaves. But, it is time for thee to turn in, it is late."

As the boys and Sarah said goodnight to their mother and father, Gabe said, "Thank thee, Father. I needed to listen to this lesson." To himself Gabe thought, 'Violence is always wrong. Even a slave owner may find his own inner light again and repent. I am not his judge, but I can be his guidance as Woolman was.'

Gabe, Rafe, and Sarah headed upstairs. Gabe fell asleep quickly, thanking the Lord that he had a father, especially a father like his. Rafe lay there for some time, thinking about what Tucks had told Gabe about slavery. He decided there and then that he would follow Woolman's example and convince others of the evil slavery held for the slave and for the master. Sarah too had listened, and held all those words in her heart.

Sailing Ships

A few days later, Tucks came up quietly and sat down next to Gabe as he drew. "Let's take a look at those sketches now." After looking at them closely, Tucks said, "Much better. Now lad, it's time for another lesson."

Gabe had hoped for a continuation of the earlier story, but was willing to learn more about the ships instead, if that was what Tucks wanted.

"We will talk about the kinds of sailing ships there be. Remember, the sloop usually has one mainmast, though it could have two, and the sails are set behind the masts so they can be moved to catch any breeze. The mainsail on the sloop is attached to a gaff at the head, and a boom at the foot. Above the gaff a tops'l can be set. So, in this sketch, you need a gaff, like a slanted branch holding the top of the mains'ls and the bottom of the tops'l. Draw it slanted between the two sails. The bottom or mains'ls is straight along the mast, and along the boom at the bottom, so draw a straight line there."

Gabe looked confused, so Crispus Attucks explained. "Think of the boom as a straight branch, that holds the bottom of the sail in place. There is also a boom on a jib, or triangular-shaped sail, which goes on the opposite side of the mast, toward the prow of the ship. It catches the breeze and can make the sloop speed across the water.

"This ship with two or three masts is called a schooner. Notice, it is larger than a sloop. It is rigged similarly, with mainsails and topsails, gaffs and booms that move to catch the breeze, but because it is larger, a

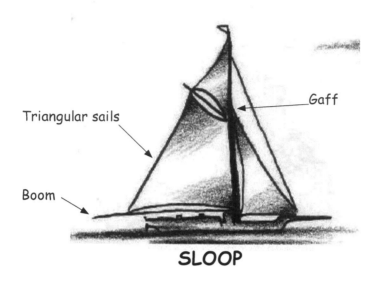

Triangular sails

Gaff

Boom

SLOOP

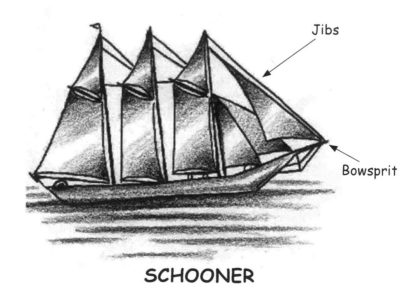

Jibs

Bowsprit

SCHOONER

schooner can have more jibs on the bow. I have seen some with four or five masts, but none here in Boston.

"A brig has two masts, fore and main which be fully square-rigged. Square-rigged means ..."

"The sails are usually rectangular and cannot be moved to catch the wind, like on sloops or schooners," Gabe interrupted.

"Right. Good work, lad. Now, the mainmast of a brig carries a fore and aft sail. This makes it handier to catch the breezes, so a brig is more maneuverable than a regular square-rigged ship, but not as handy as a sloop or a schooner. A brig can also carry two jibs.

"A brigantine is like a brig. It has two masts. The foremast is square-rigged like the brig, but the mainmast carries a large fore-and-aft mainsail, above which it can carry a main-tops'l, and a topgallant sail. These be hung on yards which be straight spars which cross the masts.

"The other square-rigged ships be called the ship, the bark, or the barkentine. I know it sounds strange to have a ship called a ship, but a seaman would not call a sloop a sloop ship, or a brig a brig ship. This square-rigger called ship usually has three or four masts, each composed of a lower-mast, top-mast, and top-gallant mast. Each mast has yards and square sails. The mizzenmast also carries a small fore-and-aft sail to assist with steering.

"The bark is similar to the ship, but the mizzenmast (aft-most) is fore-and-aft rigged, while all the other masts be square-rigged. This is the workhorse of the square riggers. I have seen a barkentine in the Pacific Ocean. They be rigged for the slightest breeze and sail in both the

Mainmast with fore and aft sails

Two square-rigged masts

BRIG

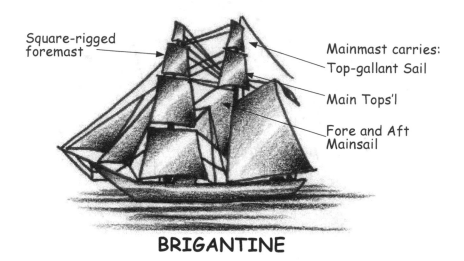

Square-rigged foremast

Mainmast carries:
Top-gallant Sail

Main Tops'l

Fore and Aft Mainsail

BRIGANTINE

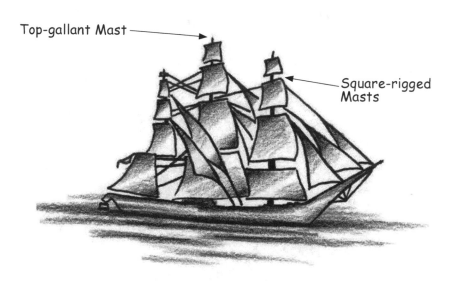

Top-gallant Mast

Square-rigged Masts

SHIP

Mizzenmast
Fore and Aft Rigged

BARK

Square-rigged
foremast

Fore and
Aft Rigged

BARKENTINE

ocean and coastal areas. A barkentine often has four or five masts, though I have seen some with three. The foremast is square-rigged, while all the other masts be fore-and-aft rigged. This gives it more maneuverability than other square-riggers.

"When the ships be in harbor, it can be difficult to notice all the little details, but like your father said, details be important. Be sure to notice the yards and rigging, look for the gaffs and booms, the bowsprits, and yards."

Gabe said, "I think I have that all down in my journal. Where did thee have to climb that first day out, when thee did not know anything?"

Crispus Attucks laughed—a good laugh, hearty and cheerful. "I would have thought you had enough of ships today. You will be correcting sketches for some time."

When Gabe looked disappointed, Tucks said, "Okay. We have time.

"In the midst of that storm, and not knowing what I was to do, I had to climb to the top of the mainmast, and let down the tops'l. The added difficulty was that the topsails be on slanted gaffs, and the mast does not go all the way up, instead there is an extra mast that fits on top of the mainmast that holds the tops'l. This mast can be removed, but a rope ladder must be climbed to lower the tops'l, then the tops'l has to be furled and fastened to the gaff so it will not flap around and tear, of course all the while the wind is whipping and the ship is listing first to one side then to the other, and the sail wants to flap around your face before you get it lashed down.

"It be a frightening time. The wind blowing, the enormous waves— white capped, like snow-covered mountains—slapping the ship around and foaming over the deck, the ship all the time riding up one mountain and down the other side. Sometimes it looked like the mountains of water would overwhelm us, and then the ship would rise up another peak. All the time, things were tumbling, the cargo shifting, and water casks rolling from side to side. And the frightening sounds, the cables screeching in the pulleys and tackles, the wind howling through the shrouds, the clacking of the chain pumps, the darting rays of lightning, and thunder so loud we could not hear each other. The air smelled like sulfur, and then the Crack! of a mast breaking. Seamen scurrying to hatchet the frayed, tangled rigging to release the broken mast, now slamming against the sides of the ship, before it did damage, or caught some poor soul in its grasp, and all the time I was clinging to the ropes and trying to work."

Gabe asked, "Is it always so frightening up in the masts?"

"No. At least not for me, and I do not think it be for most seamen. You be up there to do work, and the ship and crew depend on you for their lives so you do not have time to be afraid. On the other hand, on a calm day skimming along with the trade winds, it be the only place to sit. There be always, well almost always, a breeze up top and the sea glistens."

"What happens when there is no breeze?"

"Well, sometimes we wait for a breeze, other times we sail by ash breeze."

"What is that?"

"Well, lad, sailors tie a rope to a boat, and other seamen row hard pulling the ship along. Since the oars are made of ash wood, we call it sailing by ash breeze."

"That seems like really hard work. It is difficult to imagine rowing strong enough to pull a ship," Gabe said.

Crispus replied, "There be many things at sea that a landsman could not imagine. Sometimes at night, the sea has a glowing river of life. If you dip a net into the glow, you bring up tiny creatures. 'Phosphorescence,' the captain calls it. Oh, there be many wonders in the sea. On other nights, sometimes just after a storm, all the ship will glow. Once I saw the captain run his hands through the glow to show us not to be frightened. He called it St. Elmo's Fire." Tucks paused, thinking his own thoughts.

"Now, that be enough for any boy, on any day …Well, it will be evening soon. Time for supper." He paused, looked at the sea, glad he had a berth, and walked away.

Gabe had much to remember, and much to write in his journal. He thought, 'Each day with Tucks is like a day at school. I wonder what else he will teach me when he returns from his next voyage?'

As Tucks walked home that late afternoon, John Watson waved him over. John had the idea that if he hung canvas on the sides of the summer kitchen, Mary would be protected from the cold and bad weather as she did the laundry. Mary's reputation was such that more and more wealthy homes and businesses were sending their dirty linen to her, and she washed in all sorts of weather. The Watsons needed the income she brought to support four adults and three children, and John would do anything to improve conditions for his lovely wife. Crispus Attucks was thankful to have something physical to do after sitting so long with Gabe. He was even more thankful for the stew he shared with John after they completed the work.

Tucks got anxious after too long at shore. Luckily he would be shipping out the next day, information he had shared with Gabe and now shared with John. John promised to look after the small cabin for Tucks while he was on a short journey to the Indies.

Summer 1767

In the Print Shop

Tucks had been gone for a month this time, and Gabriel wondered when he would see his friend again, as he still had lots of questions to ask. Gabe's health was up and down. He was still weak, though browning in the sun. The salt air seemed to restore his spirits, but even after a day soaking warmth on the top deck of the *Intrepid*, he still went home to a nap before supper.

Supper conversations were livelier these days. The British had set up a Board of Customs Commissioners in Boston, and Parliament had passed another set of taxes, the Townshend Revenue Acts. These new regulations taxed paper, tea, glass, lead, and paints, which really cut into Father's printing business profits. Paper and lead could be hard to come by in good times, since most of these supplies came from London. Now, the British were making things more costly. There was talk about reinstating the boycott on British goods. Father feared more mob violence. The Sons of Liberty were talking loudly about taxation and representation. Although Father had jobs to print, it was harder to find the means to do so; while he could mold-cast replacement letters from lead and antimony, it was time-consuming work.

As the school year ended, it was time for Rafael to start his apprenticeship. It would not be a true apprenticeship, for Rafe would not be bound to Father, but he would become a journeyman printer at the end of seven years.

Father had one press. As a job printer, he printed laws, proclamations, sermons and other theological papers, blank forms for business and law, a few chapbooks or pamphlets, and primers, as well as broadsides, advertisements, and ballads. There had been a growth in population and the reading public in Boston. His print shop was busy, there were always sale posters, theater announcements, personal declarations, elegies, amateur poetics, political statements, and more to print. Between major jobs, they printed tickets, bills of lading, letterheads, government forms, and the like. There was always government work to print, including military commission forms and colonial financial forms.

The print shop was a gathering place for a variety of people. It was a center for information and the latest news, as well as a place for people to purchase their stationery needs, letters, magazines, and newspapers. The shop occupied the front half of the building. The building's back half contained the family's living quarters, with the loft rooms above for sleeping.

The front third of the shop was separated from the rest by a counter that contained samples of work. Between the counter and the shop door were movable benches where men gathered to read or talk. The shop door was in the center of the front facing the street. On either side of the door were wide windows that let in sunlight. The door and the windows had strong wooden shutters that could be locked shut in bad weather and times of danger. On each of the side walls were narrow windows, equally shuttered, that let in early-morning and late-afternoon light.

The back side of the counter had shelves holding supplies, work to be done, and completed work to be picked up or delivered. The back two thirds of the shop contained the one large press. A stove stood in the middle of the room, and lamps hung with pulleys could be raised to the ceiling on cloudy days, or early evenings. Along the back wall were cabinets of typefaces and decorative molds.

Rafe found his new position to be an exciting one. He learned printing was as much art as science. He would have to learn to space letters and lines so they were easy to read and pleasing to the eye. He would have to be careful in spreading the ink on type so the letters would not blur. Charles taught him how not to be heavy-handed. That Charles had just finished his apprenticeship was a blessing for Rafe, as Charles remembered all the mistakes he had made and could pass on the information so that Rafe wouldn't lose time making the same mistakes.

Rafe's first assignment would be to select the letters from the storage case, arrange them in words and lines, lock them into place in an iron frame called a chase, then put the chase on the press. This was not the easy task it seemed. First, for each word and line, the compositor or typesetter would gather the type sorted by letter, size, and style. Then he would pick up a single letter from a tray of type and place it upside down on an iron rule called a composing stick. The letters forming words and lines would need to be set backward since printing reversed the image. This was the first of many tricks of the trade Charles shared. As a typesetter, Rafe would have to learn to read the text he set upside down and backward.

When several lines were completed, they were set in wooden cases called galleys. The galleys were tied with string, gathered and locked in a page-sized iron frame, or chase, and secured to the stone bed of the press. A carriage carried the chase back and forth beneath a pressure plate, or platen.

Next, working as the "beater," using wood-handled, wool-stuffed, leather-covered ink balls, Rafe would spread a mixture of varnish and lampblack evenly on the type. Moistened sheets of paper were laid in a cushioned frame that hinged down on the chase, and the carriage was run in. Mounted on a screw, about the size of a man's forearm and operated by a long-handled lever, the platen was lowered by the pressman, or puller.

Each sheet was squeezed against the type under about two hundred pounds of pressure to receive its impression, and then set aside to dry before the other side was printed. Each impression required about fifteen seconds. The workday lasted up to fourteen hours. An efficient beater-puller team might produce 180 to 240 sheets an hour. For Rafe, the days were long and hard. Father and Charles were demanding, but Rafe understood he had much to learn, and the longer he took to learn, the longer Charles would feel the need to put off getting his first good paying job. Father could not afford to pay Charles what he could earn in a larger firm, and a feeling of guilt pressed Rafe to learn quickly.

A talented printer might develop an eye for attractive layout, design, and typography. In this, Rafe excelled. Like Gabe, Rafael had an eye for detail. Rafe attracted attention to their printed pieces by specially designed woodcuts he made himself in the evenings. He learned the trade quickly, as though he were born to it. The irony was that he was excelling in writing, spelling, reading, and sums—though not for a schoolmaster, but for a living.

Rafe was also learning much more. He was an avid listener of the conversations in the print shop about taxation, and the threat of a Parliament choosing to severely tax a people too far away to directly protest or vote. The only choice was to prevent the tax from being collected here. This was only logical, it seemed to Rafe. But how to prevent the tax collection without the violence? The colonial assemblies had no power over the collectors, and colonial judges could only do so much. It was a problem, and one the Sons of Liberty had a solution for: armed conflict. While the majority of the people seemed to want to work things out with the King, there was also a growing feeling that the King did not want to work things out with the colonists. Rafe feared the possible violence of the days ahead. The influence of John Dickinson's *Farmers' Letters* might lead the way, with its focus on common problems, a common cause, and an "independent" attitude. In 1765, Dickinson had written essays protesting the Stamp Act. He argued that it would be bad economics to tax the colonies in that way, and as Father had said, it would most severely hurt the poorest of the colonists. Rafe remembered part of the essay that said many countries had lost control of their people though harshness, but none through kindness. So from the first, Dickinson seemed to be warning Great Britain of the danger her taxation of the colonies could have.

In 1767, he wrote again. This time, in "Letters from a Farmer in Pennsylvania," his words were stronger. He wrote that Parliament did not have the authority to tax America, as it was not and could not be represented in the House of Commons, an ocean away. He went so far as to assert that Parliament had absolutely no right to tax the colonies. And if Parliament succeeded in taking money from the colonies, we had no liberty at all. Dickinson did maintain that Parliament had the right to regulate trade between Great Britain and her colonies. And this regulation of trade was "essential and necessary for the common good of all."

Rafe was pleased that Dickinson had a moderate tone. So many of those who spoke or argued in the print shop, like Sam Adams and James Otis, claimed Parliament had no claim on the colonies at all. Rafe wondered about Adams and Otis, and their unsettling history. First there was James Otis, a brilliant politician, but one who lately seemed mentally unstable. One day he would preach liberty, and the next lecture about colonial duty to the mother country.

At first, Adams had been Otis's right-hand man, but now Otis seemed to lean on Adams, who was clearly the one in charge. How had this happened? Sam Adams, from all Rafe had heard, was a bit of a ne'er-do-well, despite being one of the few to earn a Master's degree from Harvard College. Adams first job was in a counting house, where he lasted only a month. When placed in charge of his father's business, he let it go to ruin. He had been placed in charge of collecting taxes, and had let many get in arrears. Adams was so poor at one time that his neighbors supplied him with food for his two children. He was no businessman, but he was a great orator and writer. No one could articulate the issues of the time like Sam Adams. 'How ironic, he can explain the economics of Parliament's taxes, and could not run his own household,' Rafe thought. 'But then, who am I to judge? When I look at my own condition, I have much to regret. Am I not a Quaker? Should I not be in favor of supporting the King's requests? Instead, I have not chosen to resign from involvement in politics, as our brethren in Pennsylvania have, but instead embroil myself in the arguments. I have much to consider. I am not trying to convert others, nor do I speak out in the street, nor do I long for martyrdom, as the early Quakers did when they came to Massachusetts. Father said the Lord does not demand this of us, and that it is better to live for God than to die for him, better and harder. Even our language is changing, and Father says we must change with it. Plain speech is better and more loyal to our beliefs than all the words with fancy endings.

'Beliefs,' Rafe thought. 'What of my beliefs? I feel so much anger against the British and all they have done and are doing against the poor, and against small businessmen. It is the small businessman who is harmed with all of the new taxes, and we have no choice but to pass the cost onto our customers. Enough of that. Why should I feel anger? Should I not accept these burdens as from God, like Job? But if I don't believe in violence, then how do I protect those I love? Must I be willing to sacrifice my family, as the Quakers in Pennsylvania sacrificed the Western settlers? No, Father says that is wrong thinking. The Western settlers were killed by the Indians because the Quakers didn't understand that the real problem was the tribes losing land as it filled with settlers. If the real issue had been dealt with, perhaps the killing would have been avoided. He says the ultimate question is how much do I love God and believe in His will for my life? I don't have an answer yet. How can I purify myself if I can't answer this important question? And, despite attending meetings, I am not sure I am fully Quaker. And, if not Quaker, what am I?'

1768

Tucks Returns

While thirteen-year-old Rafe spent his days with Father in the print shop, eleven-year-old Gabe spent his time on the *Intrepid*. He baked in the sun and watched the harbor, or lay in the shade of the slave deck and corrected his sketches or read. He met with the schoolmaster once every two weeks. Gabriel knew in his heart he would not return to school in the fall as he had hoped, but Father had arranged for the schoolmaster to tutor Gabe one afternoon a week when school began again, and later to have him attend school half days as his health improved.

It was great to be able to concentrate on reading; it had been several months since he had been able to spend more than a few minutes at a time with pen or book. Having to sketch ships and attend to detail had helped Gabe develop his attention span. Writing what Tucks had said had helped sharpen his memory. Gabe wondered how Tucks was doing. Were there storms, or shipwrecks? The men on the docks seemed nervous these days, but Gabe was too tired to ask why. He just wanted life to get back to normal again. Gabe longed for the day when he would not need long naps before supper, and when he could do chores and be useful again.

At supper one evening, Rafe and Father were excited about a pamphlet they had read, "Consideration on Slavery." Written as if it were a letter addressed to a friend, the author remained anonymous. Father had heard that Nathaniel Appleton, who worked with James Otis, had written the pamphlet, but this had not been confirmed. Other minds, like the

Society of Friends, were informing the public of the evils of slavery, and asking: How can we ask for freedom, when we enslave others?

In March, the people of Boston pressured the Legislature to prohibit the further importation of slaves, which increased the conversation on both sides of the issue. While no action was taken, the direction against slavery seemed clearly set in motion. Gabe could hardly wait to tell Tucks the good news, and to share a story from Father demonstrating how our "peculiar people" reacted to threats of violence.

Tucks was often gone for months at a time. In April of 1768, when Tucks returned, he seemed out of sorts; thinner and darker. Gabe and he just sat together for some time, watching the nearest sloop ride up and down on the swells. Gabe thought there must have been a storm in the Atlantic for the harbor to be so choppy. Then he smiled to himself. 'A year ago I would not have thought twice about ships or harbor waves.'

Tucks broke the silence. "Right. Now, let me see that journal of yours."

Gabe handed it over, and Crispus Attucks looked at the illustrations. "Much, much better. Take a look at that rigging here; note the directions of these lines. These be not to control sails but to support the masts. Remember, tall masts cannot support themselves; they need lines to keep them in position, especially in storms. There, that be better. You have really improved your attention to detail!"

"Coming from thee, that is a great compliment!" said Gabe. "How was thy voyage?"

"It not be a good one, lad. Two weeks out, we met a British warship short of crew. Several of us be pressed into service. When we reached Nantucket, I jumped ship to return to Boston. Serving on a British naval ship is the worst experience I have had as a seaman. As I told you before, the Captain be lord of the ship. He holds the safety of his crew in his hands, and their lives. I cannot speak for British warships in general, but if this voyage is any example, I never want to serve on one again. I saw four men whipped with forty lashes each, then doused with saltwater."

"What had they done?" asked Gabe.

"As far as I could see, lad, their only crime be not moving fast enough to orders. Maybe they had a history of shirking, I do not know, but their punishment be brutal. Afterward, some of their messmates rubbed a salve into the stripes on their backs, and despite their wounds, they had to stand the next watch. That is enough about that. What have I missed?"

Gabe told Tucks about the anti-slavery articles and the instructions to the Legislature. Tucks listened and said he had heard it all before and did not believe anything would come of it. "The only people doing anything about slavery be you peculiar people with your peculiar way of talking."

Gabe thought, 'Tucks is really negative today. Maybe a story will cheer him up.' "Want to hear a story my father taught me about us peculiar people?"

"That would be nice. I've been telling all the stories so far," Tucks said.

"My father calls it 'Fierce Feathers.' One day, the Friends were at a meeting. Oh, I should explain first. Friends usually have a meeting, or go to church, twice a week. Only we have no ministers. We sit quietly with each other until someone feels moved to speak or pray, and then he or she shares. If no message comes that day, we simply sit for the time and then leave."

"Gabe, that be peculiar. No one runs the meeting? No minister? How be it like church then?"

"We believe in the value of silence for encouraging meditation and fellowship. I do not know how to explain it, but it is a holy quiet. Thee feels the presence of God, even if no one speaks. Any business is handled in Monthly, Quarterly or Yearly Meetings. At these meetings, committees get together, with elders and a clerk, for worship and to discuss issues of concern. No vote is taken on these issues, instead the discussion is a free exchange of ideas. The clerk writes the consensus reached on each issue and then reads the writing back to the gathering to ensure approval. If no consensus is reached, an issue is postponed. Even the meetings begin and end in silence, as does the worship.

"Getting back to the story ... the Friends were at a meeting when two Indian Braves passed the open window, then two more. Next a leader, the chief, stood in the doorway. One by one, the Friends noticed the presence of the Indians. Thee have to understand, there is no way a Friend would take a weapon into a meeting, not a gun, or sword, or weapon of any kind. This time was no different, except this time they seemed to be in danger.

"One of the men in the meeting signaled people to continue in silence, and in prayer. The Friends were nervous, as thee can imagine not knowing what to expect, but they were also calm, knowing that whatever happened would be God's will. So, they continued in silence and prayer for what seemed like a long time."

"And?"

"And, one by one, each brave laid his weapon on the ground, entered the cabin, and sat silently with the Friends at prayer," Gabe concluded.

"That be a great story. I wish all white men treated Indians without violence. I have a story like that too, but it does not have such a happy ending, at least not for the Indians. Remember asking about my mother's family?"

"Yes," said Gabe.

"Well, they be Natick Indians," Tucks said.

Wampanoag

"Today some would call them Wampanoag, if there be any left. At any rate, the story goes like this: Before any Europeans came, there be an Indian giant called Moshup. He once lived on the mainland of what now be Massachusetts, and settled on the island of Martha's Vineyard. He loved to sit on top of a hill near a town now called Gay Head. You can still see the depression where he sat.

"Moshup loved to eat whale meat. He would throw stones into the water to step on and catch the whales with his hands. That be how the rocks between Cuttyhunk and Devil's Bridge came to be. He would cook the whale meat over a fire he made from trees he ripped from the ground. That be why there are so few trees in the Gay Head area.

"He loved the Indians who lived near him, and shared his meals with them. So, one year, the Indians gathered all the tobacco they grew and gave it to Moshup. It barely filled his pipe. After smoking, he emptied the ashes into the water, and that be what formed Nantucket Island.

"One day he shared a prophecy with the Indians. Moshup said that in the future, some pale-faced men would come to their land. When they arrived, these pale-faced people should not be allowed to land. If they did, Indians would live no more.

"Moshup soon moved to another place. When the pale-faced men arrived, the Indians showed them friendship, and let them stay. You can see for yourself the results." As Tucks finished his story, he looked at Gabe. "Not the ending you hoped for, be it?"

Gabe gulped, and said, "No, it was not. It seems thee had much to hate in the white man."

"Perhaps, but I have learned the hard way that hatred does not get me anywhere, and revenge on a whole people is not possible. Despite all their problems with white men, and the problems black men have faced, my mother's tribe be not very welcoming to me once I became a man."

"Why not?" Gabe asked.

"I think they be afraid I would marry one of the girls, and there be so few pure Natick."

"That they did not want thee spoiling the purity?" Gabe finished.

"I guess I understand that, but I do not understand why they did not listen to Moshup, and then discouraged me."

"They should have listened to Moshup."

Tucks continued. "Yes, they should have listened to Moshup, for the history of my mother's people demonstrates the good and bad that happened because they did not listen. My full name is Crispus Attucks. My mother, Nancy, was a direct descendant of John Attucks, who was murdered at the end of King Philip's War. The victors would say he was executed for treason, but treason against whom? He fought for his people.

"It happened almost a hundred years ago, but it be fresh in my mind today. My mother told me the story many times, and I have heard different versions from the storytellers of the village. But I like my mother's version best.

"The many tribes were organized into a confederation—something you colonists will have to do if you intend to form your own country. Over the confederation be a head sachem. The English called them kings, hence King Philip's War. But the sachems be not kings like the British kings. Sachems had to consult with counselors of their tribes, as well as the influential people in their tribes, before making a decision that affected the tribe. Men or women could be sachems, and became sachems because of their birth, success in battle, wisdom, and leadership.

"Shortly after the English arrived, a plague wiped out almost ninety percent of our people. Many tribes lost land, and sachems lost power. But the Wampanoag remained welcoming to the English, even helping them survive the long first winter, and showing them how to plant in this unfamiliar land. In return, more English arrived who were not as friendly. Tribes were forced to move further and further west, and more and more sickness spread, and fewer and fewer of our people survived.

"A change came with a man called John Eliot. My mother always spoke lovingly of him, though he came to the tribes many years ago. He was the one to bring Christianity to the tribes, as well as reading and writing. My mother always thought the tribes chose change as a way to survive, to become Englishmen; which be why they moved to special areas called praying towns."

Gabe looked pleased until Tucks continued. "But we would never be English enough. I know we would always be Indian, and less. One of the sachems was named Massasoit. He had two sons, and wanted them to have English names, so they were named Alexander and Philip. Alexander be the oldest, and when Massasoit died, Alexander became sachem in his place. He was called to visit Plymouth to meet with the English, and died on the way home. My mother said he be poisoned; the English said he died of fever. At any rate, Philip became sachem.

"Now, Philip be a clever man. He understood the English—maybe you colonists be learning to understand them too. Even though, in my story, you be the English. At any rate, Philip knew that if the tribes continued as they be, the English would take over all their land, and the remaining Indians would become English themselves. They would give up their culture, their way of life, and their religion, as many, like my mother's ancestors, had already done. So, Philip decided to find a way to slow down the English advance.

"Philip had a big problem: numbers. There be only one thousand Wampanoag Indians but some thirty-five thousand colonists. Even if all the different tribes in the area joined Philip, they would only have fifteen thousand on their side. Perhaps the colonists realized what lay ahead, for they called Philip and others to Taunton. There he be accused of plotting against the colonists, and forced to sign an agreement for the Wampanoag to give up their weapons. Philip, remembering his brother's death, did not stay for the meal, and did not turn over any weapons to the colonists.

"The English continued to seize land, and other tribes chose to ally themselves with Philip. Then, the body of John Sassamon was found. It was rumored that Sassamon had warned the English of danger and of Philip's growing number of Indian allies. Three Indians be accused of his murder and be hung. Philip was warned that the English were trying to capture him, and that was enough to start the war.

"The English who lived with the Christian Indians felt they would not be attacked. But, over time, mistrust forced them to move the Christian natives to Deer Island in Boston Harbor. My mother told me great suffering awaited them. The people had chosen to become what the

English wanted: they became Christians, they learned to read and write, and lived as the English. But now that there was trouble, the English did not trust their converted Christians, so they were sent away to an island with limited game and insufficient clothing in the heart of winter. Many of these people died. Some escaped to fight.

"The war spread from Massachusetts all over New England. Unfortunately it be a bad winter. The English had food, but the warring tribes had little time to gather it. Then Philip's strongest ally, Sachem Canochet of the Narragansett, was captured and executed, his body quartered and put on public display. That next fall, the English found Philip and his people. Philip escaped, but the English captured Philip's wife and nine-year-old son and sold them as slaves in the West Indies. Late in August, Philip be shot and killed. They hung his head at Plymouth for twenty years. Only four hundred Wampanoag survived. Those who had been captured in war were sold to slave traders. Others were forced to move to Natick and other of Eliot's praying towns. Here, under Eliot's protection, they prospered, but almost half of all the remaining Indians in New England were killed in the war or starved from hunger, and John Attucks was hung," Tucks finished sadly.

"They should have listened to Moshup," Gabe said.

"Yes, they should have listened to Moshup. But then we would not be friends, would we?" You know, some people call us 'Children of the Morning Light.' That is like you peculiar people. I have heard you called 'People of the Inner Light.'"

"It is like we are kindred spirits or something," Gabe said, amazed.

"Or something," Tucks smiled. "Well, it be getting late. Almost time for supper."

"I will be seeing thee," said Gabe.

"I will be seeing thee," smiled Tucks.

That evening, Father read Gabe's journal carefully. What a history lesson his son was gaining, although Father's family had told the story a little differently.

His grandparents had known John Eliot in England when Eliot was a boy. All who knew Eliot expected him to enter the clerical world, as his devotion to God was evident even as a child. The Bellson family lost track of him when they immigrated to the colonies. Later they heard he was in Massachusetts, and was a missionary to the Indians. Eliot was so successful, that Parliament incorporated the "Society for the Propagation of the Gospel in New England" which supported him.

His first Christian Indians moved from Nonatum to Natick, the first Christian Indian town, where they had homes, a meeting house, and a schoolhouse. Eliot preached to them whenever he was able, once every two weeks as long as he lived. A second town was established at Ponkapog, now known as Stoughton. Others took up his methods and in twenty short years there were four thousand Christian Indians, the Puritans called them "praying Indians," and their homes "praying towns."

But even more than his conversions, was the work Eliot did to educate the Natives. He created an Algonquian alphabet, and then translated the Bible and later a Catechism into that language. In fact, the first Bible printed in the New World was in the Algonquian language, a language the various Indians of Southern New England shared. Once the Natives had their own alphabet and works in their own language, they were on their way to literacy. Eliot agreed to learn their spoken language, and the Natives agreed to learn the Western world's phonetic alphabet. A few of the Christian Indians even attended Harvard College, and yet the disaster that lay ahead almost destroyed everything.

'Violence begets violence,' Matthew thought as he remembered the story.

The English, the Puritans, had not been kind to the Natives—Tucks's mother got that right. The English had done much worse to the Natives than in the story she told, despite the fact that old Massasoit had been the reason the Puritans did not die that first winter.

Matthew remembered, 'From what my father and grandfather told me, the Puritans did everything they could to get title to Indian land. They imposed absurd fines, so a Native would have to forfeit his land to pay them. They allowed livestock to run wild and ruin Indian crops, so the Natives would leave voluntarily. They also threatened violence if a Native would not sell, or would get a Native drunk so he would not know he was signing away the deed to his land.'

Matthew's grandfather had been angered at the treatment of Natives during the war, and told Matthew of the massacred Narragansett and Wampanoag at the Great Swamp in South Kingstown, especially the burning of wigwams where women and children were trapped. Some of the worst killings were of native women and children trying desperately to run from the battles, or trying to surrender. His grandfather had said that many of those who survived the war were sold into slavery in the West Indies to help pay for the war.

Of course there had been bloodshed on both sides. More than half the towns in New England had been attacked. In the Massachusetts Bay Colony only three settlements remained, others had been destroyed or abandoned. But despite the six to eight hundred dead Englishmen, three of every twenty Indians had been killed—more than 3,500. Matthew's grandfather liked to quote a man who described Philip as "a patriot attached to his native soil ... a prince true to his subjects, and indignant of their wrongs ... a soldier, daring in battle, firm in adversity, patient of fatigue, of hunger, or of every variety of bodily suffering, and ready to perish in the cause he had espoused. Proud of heart, and with an untamable love of natural liberty ... with heroic qualities and bold achievements that would have graced a civilized warrior." His grandfather would say, "After listing the qualities of a Greek God, why would the man come back with 'civilized warrior'? Why did he feel Philip was not civilized? Because he fought back for his people?"

Father thought, 'We have so much to answer for as men who claim to be Christians. God gave us this country, and what have we done to it and to the kind people who helped us get settled our first years here in the wilderness? Ah, Gabe, you are gaining a history lesson that few your age will learn.' As he mused on his family, there was a knock at the door.

He let in Sam Adams. Before Adams had a chance to explain his order, there was another knock on the door. Matthew opened it to find the usual messenger from Hutchinson. The man walked in, ignored Sam Adams, and bluntly said, "This is to be printed first thing. The Governor needs the papers for the General Court at noon tomorrow! Anything else," he said looking at Adams, "can wait." Then the messenger strode out the door.

Adams looked at the printer and said, "Well, we better put my 'tirade' on the bottom of the stack, right?"

Father sighed, looked at the papers from Hutchinson's messenger, then turned to Adams and said, "Sam, what can I do for you."

Adams replied kindly, "More to the point, what can I do for you? What's in Gabe's journal this time?"

"King Philip's War. It seems Tucks is really an Attucks, like you thought, and his mother descends from the praying Indians. She told her son the story, and today he told Gabe the story. Seems like sadness all around."

"It was a sad time, that's for sure. Did you know that part of the mess we're in now with Parliament stems from that time?"

Father said, "What do you mean?"

Adams smiled and said, "And you the man who says violence begets violence." He went on to explain, "First, of course, the war began over the treatment of Natives, but especially over the killing of a young brave, shot by misunderstanding. Second, Massachusetts's colony lost a lot of prestige with England over the handling of the war, and the charter was changed. When Parliament heard the reports and complaints of Northern New England, over the way Massachusetts treated the Natives, they changed the charter, and ended the confederation of New England. In its place, they created the Dominion of New England under a royal governor, Andros. He lost his position during the Glorious Revolution, but at Andros's departure, a new charter was introduced. Now, Massachusetts would have a governor appointed from England, and voting rights would be determined by ownership of property, rather than religion. So, Massachusetts reaped violence to its liberty, and lost control of its governance. It will take a long time to return to the freedom we once had."

Father looked at Adams, who was no longer smiling, and said, "Yes, violence begets violence. Please, do not forget it, Sam."

As Sam Adams walked out of the shop, Father sighed. He too had learned a history lesson this evening.

Elusive Hope

"Tucks, I was thinking about your story yesterday. Thee spoke of getting to know the British, and form a confederation and gain independence. What did thee mean by all that?" Gabe asked.

Tucks began slowly. "I guess I be pretty negative yesterday, but I overheard conversations on the British warship that changed my mood. They said that a Major General Thomas Gage be looking for a fight with the colonists. Particularly with us here in Boston. I heard them quote Gage as saying all he needed was a legal pretense to collect an army which might stop us colonists from making audacious threats about taking up weapons. Audacious threats? How could our small numbers defeat the great British, with all their warships and troops? It would be like King Philip's War all over again."

Gabe asked, "What art thee saying? Gage would start a war against Boston?"

Tucks replied, "Yes, lad. That be exactly what I think he wishes to do. All he needs is an excuse. Gage also assumes those who favor the King will rise up against the others in Boston. And, if that happens, Gabe, the time may come when we will not be able to get together ..."

Gabe interrupted. Becoming at first pale, then agitated, and gradually feverish, Gabe croaked, "What do thee mean, we will not be together? Even if I can start school in a year, Father said he still wants me to spend warm afternoons here. We will not be so foolish as to give them an excuse. The *Intrepid* is far from everything. We can still be together!"

Tucks realized he had upset the child. He had spent so much time and shared so much of himself, he had forgotten that Gabe was still recovering. Tucks felt Gabe could not and should not be spared this reality. "The time may come when it will not be safe … no, Gabe! Let me finish. I would keep you safe if I could, but I see a time coming when I will not be able to … No, lad! Be calm! Let me tell you what I feel."

"I will listen," Gabe said, and then began to calm as Crispus Attucks told of the promise of America.

"It be different here than it be in England or Europe. Here, hope in the future is as natural as breathing. But in those places, hope is not part of daily life. There, just living be hard, and there seems no end of hard living.

"Here there be land and water, and trees and fish, and animals and farms, and shipping and growing. Growing that has no end. Land that spreads to the Pacific Ocean, and who knows what lies between this ocean and that ocean? There be sunrises and sunsets and hard work that can leave the next generation better than the previous generation. All one needs is effort, a little education, and an endless West.

"England does not understand this concept of hope and frontier, or of endless growth. They see only a land of materials and people who will make England rich. They have started with taxes. The taxes seem small, unless a person is buying the item for resale, and then the taxes eat into the tiny profit margin. Each time a ship sails from our harbors all those connected worry. Will the ship go down in a storm? Will those aboard succumb to fever and die? Will the merchants lose their investment or the families their loved ones? If any of these things happen, how will those left behind survive?

"For the English, the only question is how will the government cover the loss; how will it keep the company from going broke? After the war, the colonists thought so much would be better, instead, England was left with debts, the colonists the cause, and so the ones who pay."

Gabe said angrily, "But we fought in the war too! It did not start here; it started in Europe. Father said the war cost us a lot. Here in Massachusetts, about three in ten soldiers died in the war. And, no matter how hard we fought for them, the British considered us beneath their consideration, closed the frontier, and began a series of taxes. But, we showed them, we stopped the taxes."

"Yes," Tucks said sarcastically, "we stopped the taxes all right. But that be not how the English see it. Parliament believes they did us a kindness in removing the Sugar Act and the Stamp Act, but made it a point in the Declaratory Act to say they had the right to tax the colonies. I have heard the captain and others speaking. They think it time for Britain to show its authority over the colonies. So, with the Townsend Acts, England is going to do just that. The British have sent their own custom collectors to make sure the tax be collected."

"But," Gabe said stoutly, "we will just refuse to pay them and protest until the taxes are removed."

"Probably," Tucks replied thoughtfully, "but this time I think the British will send warships and troops to keep order. Especially if there is mob violence as before."

"Is that what thee meant when thee said the docks would not be safe?"

"Yes—that and more. My ability to support myself may end. And I be just one of the many seamen ashore who may lose work."

"Thee could come live with us, Tucks. Father can always use extra help in the print shop."

"Yes, I am sure I could," Crispus Attucks said smiling, "but I be a sailor not a printer. And it will not just be sailors out of work. See if sailors cannot work, they cannot spend money. All those who depend on the sailors' money will have less to spend. All those who depend on those who depend on the sailors' money, will have less to spend. So, really, if one part of the colony be poor, it will spread to other parts of the colony, and everyone will have less, even print shops," Tucks explained.

"What will people do?"

"I think there will be violence and war. I do not see any alternative," Tucks replied.

"There must be another way. Father said violence only brings more violence."

"He is right, of course. Violence does beget violence, but sometimes a man has to fight, even if he does not want to. The whole colony be only as strong as its individual members."

"We will not fight. We do not believe violence is the solution," Gabe said nervously.

"I do not either, but Gabe ..." Tucks paused. He could tell Gabe was becoming agitated, and Gabe was not mentally strong enough to handle more. So, he changed emphasis from the war he knew lay ahead, to what needed to happen before war was the only answer. "Listen, Gabe. Before anything like that happens, people will petition to the King and Parliament. They will appeal even to the English people themselves. There be a lot to try before war."

Gabe said, "Yes, there is a lot to try. I bet if James Otis and Sam

Adams get their heads together, they can write a letter that will make the King and Parliament change their minds. After all, England will not want war either; they are still paying for the last one. Why do they not just tell us what they need, and see if we can raise the funds ourselves? There must be a way for us to help England with her debts and still be friends."

"I am sure you be right, Gabe. Write your ideas down now before you forget them and show them to your father this evening. He is a printer, and can change things with words." Crispus Attucks thought, 'A host of words probably will not change what is to come. What role must I play in this? I would that all people be free. I do not want this lad to be anyone's slave.'

Noticing the sun, Tucks said, "It's getting late, almost time for supper." He strolled away.

Gabe thought, 'Tucks is right; there is a lot we can do to change the King's mind. Father can help; he can change things with words.'

As he walked home, Tucks thought, 'I have to be careful. Gabe be only a boy, and an ill one at that. I have planted the thoughts, so violence will not be such a surprise. But I see no hope of avoiding war. British pride is at stake, and they do not like to be challenged by their inferiors. I wish I knew more about history. I have only the stories of my father and mother to go by. The Bible says we should not kill, yet to enter the Promised Land the Israelites had to do battle. I think that if we are to remain in this, our promised land, we too will have to fight. My name is Crispus, but I wish it were Moses, for I would fight these pharaohs who will not let our people alone.'

While Tucks and Gabe were discussing the future, John Watson and his wife were having a similar discussion. Mary had begun the conversation by thanking her husband, once again, for the canvas around the summer kitchen. Before the canvas, it had been only a covered walkway to a small shed and stove where summer cooking, especially canning, was done to avoid over-heating their home. Now, with the protective canvas sides, Mary and the girls devised a clever system organized to keep track of their laundry business.

At first, Mary and the girls had wrapped the fresh laundry in paper, tied with a string. Then, when paper became expensive, they carried the unwrapped linen through the town to their clients. This system was not satisfactory, for as the work became larger, the chance of dropping a clean piece of linen became greater. Luckily for the Watsons, it was about this time that the mothers came to live with them. The mothers began collecting willow branches, and wove makeshift baskets to carry the linen. One evening, after John had shipped out, Tucks stopped by to check on the family. He helped the mothers with their basket weaving, and taught them the special weaving techniques his mother had taught him.

Tucks often stopped by with willow and other branches, and the mothers wove larger baskets to hold the laundry, while nine-year-old Hope created name tags for each basket. Tucks built shelves to hold the baskets, and a table for folding. The stove was moved into the middle of the summer kitchen, where Mary boiled water for washing. When the weather was cold, the summer kitchen was quite pleasant, moist, and warm. When the weather was warm, the center canvas could be untied, and the breezes could blow through, cooling the girls.

The worry John shared with Mary was that of rebellion against the new taxes. As long as ships left the harbor, John, a veteran of many ships, would have work. But if mob violence broke out again, he worried about Mary and the girls. The last time the violence centered in town, but he wasn't so sure it would stay there this time, for he believed the British would send troops to regain control. If troops were sent, women might not be safe anywhere.

Mary reminded John that Tucks was close by, then realized if both men shipped out at the same time, she and the girls would have no protection. Mary said, "I will just have to do laundry for the officers, and then they will protect us."

John replied thoughtfully, "That would bring in extra income, but might you and the girls be in danger from those who felt you were aiding the British?"

Mary had no answer. She could only hope there would be no mob violence.

Neither John nor Mary slept well that night.

Words and Change

Father listened to Gabe's feverish recounting of the day's conversation with Tucks, and sent him to bed early. It seemed Crispus Attucks had heard frightening things onboard the British warship, things that did not bode well for the colonies. That the British were pressing men off ships at sea did not bode well for area merchants. When the British had press gangs ashore, the colonial ships avoided Boston harbor. 'Now what? Would there be more mob violence? And what of the Townsend Acts?' Father wondered.

He did not have to wonder long. Sam Adams knocked, and this time Father left with him so they would not be interrupted as he shared what Gabe had reported. Adams looked at Matthew and smiled. He had long been hoping for independence from England, and this new attitude of the British might just be the catalyst to arouse the colonies to action.

As Adams explained, the boycott of English luxury items was going well. New Hampshire, Connecticut, and New Jersey had endorsed the 1767 Circular Letter which listed colonial grievances and called for joint action. The Letter said: "... what a man has honestly acquired is absolutely his own, which he may freely give, but cannot be taken away from him without his consent ... the Acts made there (in England) imposing Duties on the People of this province with the sole and express purpose of raising a Revenue, (were) infringements of their natural and constitutional Rights because as they are not represented in the British Parliament, His Majesty's commons in Britain, by those Acts, grant their Property without consent." It went on to say that representation in Parliament would forever be "impracticable" because of the distance between England and America. The Letter also addressed the illegal nature of impressment, and of quartering (colonial room and board support) of British troops.

Matthew had printed copies of the entire document, and while he agreed with the statements made, he worried about the result. Would the King or Parliament get a chance to read the letter and more importantly, would they understand? Sam Adams thought to himself, 'I hope they don't understand.'

When the British customs officials arrived in March of 1768, they were greeted with insults, but not weapons, though Boston was not known for handling its custom collectors well. Aware of Boston's previous treatment of customs officers, including tar and feathers and/or property damage, these customs officials went at once to Governor Bernard to ask for naval ships to protect them. Bernard denied their request, believing it would cause a tense situation to explode. So the officials made their request to Commodore Hood, who complied. The warship *Romney* and sloop *Beaver* were to be sent to Boston Harbor. Father knew all this because he was asked to print documents by Hutchinson's aide.

After the customs officials had landed, but before the British warships could arrive, Boston held its celebration of the March 18th anniversary of the repeal of the Stamp Act. Father had not been pleased at the gathering of crowds, but there was no violence, though it had been a tense day:

At dawn on the 18th, there were drums beating and guns firing, and in the evening hundreds of men wandered the streets, threatening by their presence but not taking action. Boston remained calm for a time, and Father thought maybe colonists would be willing to give words a try. After all, in early March the customs officials had tried to bring a smuggling case against Hancock's ship, *Lydia*, but the case was dismissed for lack of evidence, or perhaps the customs officials and others feared testifying.

On May 17, a British warship, the *Romney*, sailed into the harbor. On the 23rd it moved closer to Hancock's docks, making a point about the toleration for smuggling and frightening witnesses. Father hoped the *Romney's* presence would settle the town.

While Father was hopeful, his friends Adams and Otis were itching for action, for change, for an uprising. Father could only hope that the successful action against the Stamp Act would be the extent of action against the Townsend Acts. 'This British system was a strange one,' Father thought. 'There are Governors and Assemblies, Legislatures and

Courts, who represent the people. But if the people do not like the actions they take, the people rebel. Protest mobs fill the streets until a change is made to their liking. It would be no different here than in England, or in other European countries. But no, it was different here. At least lately. The protests were not usually about the choices made locally, but those made an ocean away, in a place that did not understand or did not want to understand how the colonies were different from the home country.' Father wondered, 'Is that what our words should be saying, how we are different?'

When the sloop *Liberty* entered Boston Harbor, it unloaded its cargo of Madeira wine, though Hancock paid no duty on the cargo. Some said the customs officials were controlled so no duty was paid. Others said the customs officials were too afraid to say anything against Hancock until naval support arrived. Father was not sure where the truth lay. At any rate, in June, the *Liberty* was seized for illegal loading, and Hancock was fined for illegally unloading Madeira wine. It seemed there was no lack of evidence this time. This set off mob violence such that the customs officials pleaded to be placed under direct British protection aboard the warship *Romney*.

The British ships had already made themselves unwelcome, for they had begun impressing sailors to fill out their crews as soon as they arrived. Merchants and seamen alike protested this practice, but Governor Bernard believed the impressment was legal. How else could captains fill out the crews on British ships?

Father thought about all this violence. 'Have the British asked themselves why so many of their sailors jump ship, or why so few accept a birth on a British ship? Violence is never the answer; it ignores the underlying issues that reasonable men should be able resolve.'

Father also thought about Rafe and Gabe. 'Rafe's work in the print shop was excellent, but it meant he read the literature on both sides of any issue. The most passionate writing was done on the anti-British side, but not always the most logical or truthful. How much was Rafe being affected by this? Rafe had always been a quiet child, but now Father missed the talk at supper, and the family time after supper. Father still brought up issues, but Rafe seldom joined in.

'And then there was Gabe. How much longer could he let Gabe remain on the *Intrepid*? He had not seen Tucks around, and though Gabe's sketches and notes on ships and their movements helped the cause, Gabe was lonesome. True, the other boys would soon be out of school, but they would have chores to do, and most boys Gabe's age would be beginning an apprenticeship.'

Father also worried about Gabe's health. 'Gabe had been sick for a long time. It seemed like forever before he could sit up, or hold a quill, or the journal we gave him. The journal was the doctor's idea. He said Gabe would need something to keep himself occupied when he started to feel better. He said it would be difficult for a young boy to remain in bed as long as needed, if he were to be fully healed. The doctor was also the one who suggested the importance of sea air. Rafe was still in school then, and volunteered to bring Gabe's studies home. The tutor had said Gabe was one of his best pupils and destined for Harvard.

'School was never Rafe's strong suit. He could never "toe the crack" like Gabe, though neither of the boys ever visited the whipping post. Rafe was two years ahead of Gabe in school, though Gabe was catching up fast, until he got ill; so, Rafe promised to bring home school lessons, and help with Latin and Greek, when Gabe was ready.

'The year and a half of sun and sea air, as often as weather permitted, had made Gabe stronger. He would be able to return to school in the fall of 1768, and visit the *Intrepid* after school for notes, but something was still wrong. Gabe had never been calm like Rafe, but now he seemed agitated most of the time. The least remark would set him off into a verbal assault on the unfortunate speaker. And in the cool evenings, Gabe would not sit before the fire as before, instead, restless, he would sit then get up to pace. He raised issues like slavery and the treatment of the Indians, or the plight of the common man. He asked questions about who was out of work, what could be done for them and their families. And, unusual for Gabe, he did not really want answers to the questions he asked, questions that had no easy answers.'

Father did not understand why. When he spoke to Doctor Warren about Gabe, Doctor Warren explained the agitation could be a result of the illness, and hypersensitivity to the tension of the time. Like when the crowds rescued the sailor, Thomas Furlong, from impressment. It had happened far from the *Intrepid*, but the *Romney's* practice of great guns and small arms could be heard everywhere in town. Despite the tension in town, and as long as things were safe, Doctor Warren felt the *Intrepid*, built far from the major action of the docks, was a healing place for Gabe.

Leviathan

Gabe was thrilled when Tucks arrived early one afternoon. "I missed thee," Gabe said.

Tucks said, "It be great to see you too. You are looking as brown as a native who spends all his time in the sun. People might think we be brothers, except you have light hair. As brown as your skin be, your hair be even more blond than usual! All right now, lad. Let's see that journal of yours."

Gabe handed it over reluctantly. As usual, Tucks did not read any of the writing, unless it was labeling a ship. "You do not need me anymore for your journal, Gabe. Your sketches be excellent, and your labeling of particular ships and rigging be as perfect as it can be."

Gabe said, "Maybe, but I still need thee, Tucks."

Tucks said smiling, "I am not going anywhere, unless I get impressed on one of those warships. Almost nothing else be leaving the harbor."

"Do thee mean thee do not have work?"

"Oh, I be okay, Gabe. I have a little cabin down on the harbor banks. I do not need to work at the print shop yet. Besides, I have been working at the ropewalk some days, and other days I help out one or more merchants. There always seems to be a berth for someone who works hard!"

"I am glad to hear it. Did thee read the prophecy written by 'The American Whig'? I thought of our earlier conversation and felt it could have been written by thee," Gabe said.

Tucks read from an essay he pulled from his pocket. "You mean the one that says 'For territory we need not quarrel with any power upon earth … we have a country amply sufficient for hundreds of millions, and can spread out an inheritance from ocean to ocean, at a moderate expense of money, and without the guilty effusion of human blood'? I especially like the phrase 'without the guilty effusion of human blood.' It fits your idea, Gabe, of no violence. No one really wants violence, but sometimes we have to do what we do not want."

"Father says we do not, we can just turn the other cheek. Father likes the description of America. He says this really is a new Eden.He read from his copy of the essay: 'The benefits we enjoy from our situation, our climates, and the fecundity of the soil, are numberless, and not to be recounted. … On one side accessible to the ocean for all the purposes of commerce, on neither exposed to any dangerous vicinity, and from all foreign force that can essential disturb our repose too far removed.' Father did not like the idea of our reaching 'the highest elevation of grandeur and opulence.' But both of us liked …"

Tucks finished Gabe's thought, "I know. 'The finger of God points out a mighty empire to your sons … the land we possess is the gift of heaven to our fathers and divine providence seems to have decreed it to our latest posterity.' And that be right."

Gabe said, "Thee know us well."

"Yes, and better every day. Only I will have no posterity, no sons to inherit the land from God. I guess that be all right. Legally, Master Brown would own them. And I would not have more slaves be born in this age calling for freedom, when so few are free," Crispus Attucks mourned.

"Tucks, thee are different these days."

"I know, Gabe. But these days are different. It's hard to be my old self with the *Romney* in harbor and its fifty guns pointed toward Boston. Next, I suppose British troops will land and tent in Boston Commons." Seeing the look on Gabe's face, Tucks decided to temper his feelings. "Sorry, how would you like another story?"

Gabe responded with a smile.

"It be one of my first voyages, while I was still learning how to be a seaman. We left Nantucket on a warm April day. We knew the warmth would not last in April, but hoped to be south before any ice found us.

"We sailed for three days to a fair breeze, and then were driven off course by a storm that left ice on the mast. We got the tops'l furled before the ice hit, but the mains'ls be frozen in place. This could be danger-ous, as the sails could rip, frozen as they were. Luckily when the storm abated, the sun came out, and though we be off course, we had been driven south which helped the sails thaw. You cannot imagine the cold sleet, cutting into your face as you stand on the yards trying to furl sails, then, climbing down a rope ladder partly covered with ice.

"The days in the sun were glorious. I loved my time aloft and often rested there between watches. The focs'l be a dark, grimy place, but when the weather is bad we sleep below, and the smells of other men mixed with cooking odors be hard to take. I always preferred being aloft to being below. The heat of the southern climes bothered the other men, but not me, the sweat rolled off my body and I welcomed the sun after the sleet. From aloft I saw some marvelous sights."

"Like what?" asked Gabe.

"Well, have you heard about dolphins?"

"I have heard they are friendly to humans and unfriendly to sharks."

"You be right about that. When the sea be just right, and the ship rocking through the waves, dolphins would leap along the prow. They would follow us for many hours. Now and then, the cook would throw garbage overboard, and the sharks would follow to eat the sea life following to eat what we did not. One day, a shark charged a dolphin, which turned on the shark butting him in the side. Other dolphins joined the butting and the shark eventually swam away.

"I have seen other creatures too. Sometimes we would fish to supplant our rations. Some of the fish we caught had noses like long swords. Others would blow up into a large ball, and then let the air out and become tiny. Some creatures were dangerous, and not just a shark on the line, but jellyfish."

"How could the fish look like jelly?" questioned Gabe.

"Well, it really does not look like a fish. It looks more like a transparent hat with several long ribbons hanging down. Only these did not have bows on the end, but stingers. If a sailor caught one he had to be careful, the stingers were really painful and could cause swelling or death in some of the men," remembered Tucks. "Sometimes, after a bad storm, we would enter an island's sheltered waters to restock on fruit, and water. Other times, we had to cut trees to replace broken masts. I liked those island times. Often I could find a moment to walk on the sand or rocky beaches. I would find small pools where creatures would be trapped until the tide came in again—creatures that looked like stars, or clams, or tiny crabs living in empty snail shells. Oh, the wonder of it all!"

"Ah, I would like to see some of the creatures thee observed. What else?" asked Gabe.

"I hope you get to see the wonder, Gabe, but not as a sailor. A sailor works hard with short rations. He be always in danger of falling and drowning. He could get hurt from lifting and pulling, lose a finger or break an arm or leg on shifting cargo. His hands are burned in tarring lines. He can suffer from scurvy, rheumatism, typhus, yellow fever, ulcers, and other skin diseases. He listens to men swearing and arguing all day, and lives in dark, smelly quarters. I think it be not a career for someone who dislikes violence. But, let me tell you about whales.

"Whales be beautiful creatures. Some of the sailors say they are intelligent and can live to be sixty years old. They feed their babies milk like land creatures, or like humans. I have even heard them sing. Whales are huge mammals. When they dive, their tails flap the water last. They are so powerful a single tail slap could destroy a small boat. Sometimes they have so many barnacles attached to them they smell like land. Some whales have teeth, and other whales have something called *baleen*, soft-like fingernails close together. These whales gulp their food, then strain the water out, the baleen keeping the food in. Other whales, like the Right, can raise their flukes, or flippers, at right angles to the wind, and sail along letting the wind do the work. Blue whales be so big a small child could stand in the arteries leading to the heart, and the heart be as big as a wagon," Tucks said, his face glowing in remembrance.

"How do thee catch an animal that huge?" Gabe asked.

Tucks's face lost its glow, and grew somber. "It can be a scary thing. I did not go out in the boats at first, as I be so inexperienced. I stayed onboard, but aloft. First someone in the tops'l looks for sightings. When a whale is seen, he yells, 'Whale ahoy!' and the captain calls, 'Where away?' The lookout would reply, 'Off the port side.'

"Then it would be 'Boats away,' and part of the crew would get in a small boat yelling, 'A dead whale or a stove boat!' Some in the boat would be rowing toward the whale, others would navigate, and some would stand ready with an iron, a harpoon. An iron be like a double-barbed dart with a two-foot shank, mounted on a six-foot pole, and attached to a rope one hundred or more fathoms long. The goal be to get one or more harpoons in the whale deep enough not to come out when the whale struggled. When the whale is tired, the boat pulls alongside, and a lance is struck in deep to pierce the whale's lungs. When the whale is mortally wounded, the sailors cry, 'Chimney afire!' that be when the whale spouts blood. It would swim in circles, then die, 'fin out.' A rope would be attached to its flukes and they would tow it to the ship."

"But how can they harpoon a whale in a little boat, bobbing and twisting with the swells?" asked Gabe.

"Well lad, the harpooner would be in the prow of the whaleboat. When they go near enough to the whale, the harpooner stands up. To keep his balance, he braces his left thigh in the 'clumsy cleat,' a semicircular cut in the thwart. Once the harpoon is in, the whale takes off, like I said before. The line plays out, whizzing around the loggerhead, a wooden post at the stern. The men keep dousing the line with seawater to keep it from scorching or igniting. When the whale slows down, the harpooner and the boat handler change places, each moving from prow to stern, and stern to prow. It be always an issue to stand up in a boat. But they seemed to do it fine."

An amazed Gabe said, "It sounds like some kind of adventurous dance!"

"A dance, maybe. In practice, this be a dangerous activity. As the boat or boats near, the whale will sound, dive down deep. One has to keep a sharp lookout then, for when the whale comes up for air, you do not want to be over the spot. And, one needs to have patience, as some whales can stay under for up to thirty minutes, and a sperm whale from forty-five minutes to two hours. But if you can get close enough, this be a good opportunity to spear it. The whale, of course, does not like the lancing, so it will take off, towing the small boat behind. Or it might dive again. This too is a dangerous time. While towing the boat tires the whale and eventually causes its death, for the men in the small boat it means a fast ride, or a smashed boat, and danger.

"When the whale tires, the men in the boat take up the slack in the rope, making it harder for the whale to pull. When the whale has given up fighting, it will be towed to the ship. Tied alongside the ship, I could really see the size of the creature, often at least one half to two thirds the length of our ship. There be no way to get the entire whale aboard, so men go over the side and begin cutting strips of blubber, or whale fat; others pull the blubber aboard, cut it in sections, and haul the sections into huge pots where the blubber boils away into a greasy oil, which is stored in huge barrels and lowered into the cargo hold.

"Often with sperm whales, we would bring the whole head on board. The sperm whale has two 'barrels' in its head. One has spermaceti; the other has 'junk.' Spermaceti itself be beautiful, it is encased in a glistening substance, a semitransparent rose-tinted liquid, until it hits air, then it turns into a crystal-like waxy material. We warm it and put it in separate barrels. It is worth more than the oil. Junk in the other barrel is like spermaceti too, but has much more white stuff, and is less beautiful.

"The blubber is hard to cut. A man goes overboard and stands on the whale. He has a sharp spade with which he makes cuts. The whale is rotated and the blubber comes off in a spiral. The blubber is so heavy we bring it up with block and tackle. Then someone scores the blubber strip into 'bible leaves,' to make it easier to render into a liquid. In the early days, we would just pack away the blubber in chunks, for there was not an easy way to have a fire on deck. Later we had 'brick try works' aboard, and could render our own oil.

"Very little of the original whale be left when we finish, for at first blood, the sharks come, so we whittle away on top, while the sharks tear away at the bottom. Any man who falls would be lost to the sharks. So even the butchering of the whale be dangerous business."

Tucks stopped; the word *butchering* still in his mouth and the taste of the greasy oil on his tongue. There was no glow of remembering on his face.

Gabe had lots of questions, so when Tucks finished he asked, "Did a whale ever attack a ship? Could it sink a ship?"

Tucks answered with a smile, "I have never heard of a whale attacking a ship, but I know from the size of them, that a whale could sink a ship if he rammed it. Sperm whales in particular can be sixty feet long, and their skin is fourteen inches thick. I have seen whales with a harpoon in them turn and ram the boat chasing them. But I have never heard of one ramming a whole ship. That be an interesting question, Gabe, if whales are as smart as some folk believe they are, then maybe a whale could become the hunter." Tucks smiled at the thought of an attacking whale.

"Did thee not like whaling?" Gabe asked.

"I will tell you what lad; I would rather whale than sail on a British warship. And if it be a 'greasy trip,' my lay is great, but whaling is not like watching cattle. I know that some cattle are for milk and others for eating, but a whale be something different.

"Once a whale looked up at me with sorrowful eyes as it died. I felt such a kinship with the animal, that I hated even being part of the sailing of such a ship. Of course, I took part in the cooking, and ate whale steak, but I felt a sense of wrongness I cannot explain. Whaling is not like fishing. Fish do not seem to have a spirit, or a soul, or whatever it be that a whale has.

"I once saw a group of whales, some call it a *pod*. They were all in a circle, with their heads toward the center and their tails out. In the very center of the circle was a calf, outside the circle be a large male. Then I saw the danger. A group of killer whales. When they attacked one of the whales in the circle, the large whale came to its defense, and the other whales from the circle helped the wounded whale back in place. They maintained the circle and the killer whales finally gave up. Another time, I watched whales chase killer whales for a while, before coming back to their original spot. I have seen sperm whales with their newborn calves. I have seen the calves nursing. I have seen the rest of the pod helping the calf keep up. I have seen whales playing with each other, and fondly touching each other. Some kinds of whales travel alone. But sperm whales seem to travel in families. I would love to spend time just watching them, and following them around, without catching them.

"Maybe I have spent too much time with thee, my friend. I do not like the violence, or the violating of another anymore."

"But we need whale oil to light our lamps," Gabe said.

"Yes," said Tucks. "And a variety of other important things like perfume, and stays for women's corsets, and … ah well, lad. I have yapped on a long time. It be getting late, time for supper."

"Good evening, Mr. Crispus."

"Good evening, Mr. Gabriel."

Roses and Thistles

Rafe had listened as Gabe told of Tucks's whaling adventures. He later read that part of the journal, and had to disagree with Tucks about soulful eyes. Rafe felt no one who had looked into the big, brown, soulful eyes of a cow could deny their sense of feeling. He had watched mothers and calves, the love, the mother running her tongue over her calf in tenderness. Man has been given dominion over the creatures of the world, and since Eden, has had to work by the sweat of his brow to survive. Maybe no animal should be butchered and eaten. Rafe had once seen a cow butchered, its throat slit, body hung for the blood to drain, and then stripped of its hide and cut into pieces. He had not been able to eat beef for awhile. 'Is not it curious,' he thought, 'that we change the names of animals to eat them, beef for cow, pork for pig? Maybe Crispus Attucks had been so inexperienced, so innocent when he first saw the harvesting of whales that he was overwhelmed.' It was all beyond him, this relationship of man and animal.

On the few slow days in the print shop, Rafe had been allowed to keep Gabe company on the *Intrepid*, but these had not always been days when Tucks visited. Rafe felt a bit jealous of Gabe's friendship, but loved the print shop, and did not envy Gabe's empty and often lonely time in the sun.

On the wharf it was a gray, miserable day; misting just enough to keep a man damp if he had to be outdoors, and Crispus Attucks had to be outdoors. His conversations with the boy had set him on edge. He had almost said what he really wanted to say: Whaling was butchery, for those animals had souls. They sang, they bore their children alive, and fed them on mother's milk. He had seen them form a circle, with the children and mothers in the middle, when they were in danger. This was not the action of some dumb animal. And they breathed the very air he breathed.

The evil of whaling was nothing compared to the evil of sailing on a British ship. He had not told Gabe about the short rations, the unnecessary cruelty of the mates, or the barbarity of the captain and officers. For the officers, the men were means to an end, worse than slaves. At least a master had a financial interest in his slaves and a reason to keep them fed and alive. A ship captain had no such interest in his crew. The British had such a high sense of their position in the world. The crew members were not fellow Englishmen, even if they actually were citizens; instead they were subordinates, cattle, mules to slave and do at the officers' whim.

He had not told Gabe that he, Crispus Attucks, had been whipped. He had dared to explain to an inexperienced officer why a particular order should not be obeyed. That he, Tucks, was correct, only lessened the number of lashes, it had not eliminated them. He learned to hold his tongue as the other seamen did, and to jump ship with them when the opportunity arose.

Now, the danger was upon him. Press gangs from the British naval ships were all over the wharves, and knocking on the cabin doors of the poor. He felt the impossibility of hiding much longer at home, so thought he would try the *Intrepid*. Maybe as its sun-drenched warmth was curing Gabe, its dry impressment deck might afford safety for Tucks, and time to think.'

From the rumors he heard all through July and August of 1768, it sounded like the British would be sending troops to Boston. What that meant for him and others, Tucks did not know. But from what he heard on the docks, Hancock or Otis had called for an armed force to storm Castle William where the customs commissioners were. Boston selectmen called for all the town's weapons to be cleaned. Crispus Attucks knew what that meant, a warning to the British that the colonials would fight. 'Did not the colonials understand that a show of force would encourage the British to send even more troops? Here we are, me hiding in a boy's play boat, and the people of Boston goading the British to act. Does any of this make sense? No!'

Crispus Attucks's worst fears came to pass; the British were really sending troops. In September, Boston armed itself, and called a special meeting of all the towns in Massachusetts to decide what action to take when the troops arrived. Luckily the smaller towns called for restraint.

The troops arrived on October 1, 1768. One had to admit the soldiers presented an awesome sight as they marched down Long Wharf and up King Street, their drums beating, fifes playing, and colors flying. Their banners were spectacular. Carried on ten-foot poles, the Union Jack on top, then the regimental banners six-feet high and six-feet wide proclaimed their regiment's number embroidered on a red shield surrounded by roses and thistles. The ranks were in dress uniforms: first the soldiers in red coats; followed by the drummers in white hats and yellow jackets; and then the tall grenadiers, looking even taller in their high, miter-shaped bearskin caps fronted in red, bearing the House of Hanover's white horse badge and motto "They fear no difficulty." Even the infantrymen, who came last, were impressive in their black, white-laced, three-corner hats.

And when the troops arrived, bayonets drawn, marching down Long Wharf, no action was taken by the people of Boston. 'In fact,' Crispus thought, 'they acted by inaction.' When it came to quartering the troops, the townspeople refused to grant housing, so the soldiers were housed in warehouses, any empty buildings, or tented, as Tucks had once imagined, on Boston Common. That the town was quiet could only be a temporary event. The leaders were waiting for their petitions regarding the Townsend Acts to be read and responded to by Parliament. Until then, they were willing to rest in the status quo. In the meantime the troop ships, the frigate *Hussar*, and the ship-of-the-line *Rippon*, remained in Boston Harbor.

Gabe had returned to school part time. But there were still a few warm days this fall, when Tucks and Gabe could sit talking about what Gabe learned in school. As he listened, Crispus Attucks wished he knew more of geography. He had sailed to many ports throughout the world, but did not have a sense of the whole, only the length of ocean between one port and another.

1769

Unrest

Parliament's answer to the colonial petitions regarding the Townsend Acts was not one the Americans had hoped. Parliament saw the actions in Massachusetts as rebellious, so they passed a series of resolves that were delivered to the King. Sam Adams shared the resolves with a group of sailors. The resolves stated that Massachusetts' denial of the right of Parliament to tax the colonies was illegal and "derogatory to the rights of the Crown and Parliament." In addition, *The Curricular Letter*, originated by Sam Adams and sent to all the colonies, was an act of rebellion. Parliament called for an investigation that would bring the leaders to England for trial on charges of treason!

When Crispus heard the news he was stunned. There would be no peaceful resolution of the issues. It was either return to slavery, that peculiar British brand of slavery like that of shipboard, or war.

How could he explain to Gabe—gentle, nervous Gabe—that he, Tucks, would choose violence over slavery to the British? Those who had never sailed on a British ship could not imagine what that form of slavery meant. True, the colonists had banded together on a nonimportation agreement, but he saw little hope of this working in the long run. At some point, the Townsend Acts might be withdrawn, but another form of taxation or regulation would be placed upon the colonies until submission or war occurred.

Meanwhile, Crispus Attucks, he who had always been able to find work as he wished, was now hard pressed to find employment. There were no merchant ships leaving the harbor in need of crews. The naval press gangs had ceased their dastardly work, but the bored soldiers were taking every kind of work they could find. Even if the merchants employed the British soldiers reluctantly, they could hardly afford not to hire someone willing to work for less than half what a colonist would expect. And try as they may, civilians could not keep the soldiers out of the local taverns and markets.

If that were not enough, the soldiers and their officers seemed determined to insult the citizens of Boston. When the quartering of troops was not handled to their satisfaction, the officers began commandeering one public building after another. They drilled on Sunday mornings and their trumpets, drums, and shouted orders disturbed the Bostonians at prayer. So many soldiers deserted, that sentries were set up around town, and citizens had to respond to military challenges and prove who they were.

Crispus was happy Gabe was in school, except on warm afternoons. The streets were no longer safe, though the *Intrepid* still was. Sam Adams kept the docks informed of actions here and elsewhere. And Tucks would often read the broadsides or notices on buildings to those who could not read for themselves.

He had heard that in New York, civilians had been killed, and each time a Liberty Pole was set up the soldiers would cut it down. He had also heard about the Virginia Resolves, they seemed to echo what Adams had been saying: "no taxation without representation." When the Royal Governor dissolved the Virginia House of Burgesses, they met anyway and agreed to join the boycott of British goods. By October, New Jersey, Rhode Island, and North Carolina had decided on nonimportation of British goods. Now there were rumors that the Townsend Acts would be repealed. If so, the united colonies would disunite and return to their attitude of mutual distrust. Crispus Attucks hoped these rumors were true. It would be wonderful if the Acts were repealed without any more violence.

And there had been enough violence. The townspeople harassed the soldiers by calling them lobsterbacks, bloody backs, and cowards. The townspeople knew the soldiers could not fire at them. When the soldiers paraded, civilians who interrupted their ranks were greeted by bayonets. On the soldiers' side, resentment sometimes overflowed into fights. By the end of the year, there was real violence. A man suspected of tipping-off a customs collector was tarred, feathered, and carted through the streets for three hours. In November, a British captain told his troops, "If they touch you, run them through the body." Even though the captain was indicted for his orders, the mood of both sides was clear to anyone with eyes to see. Crispus saw, and remembered his time on a British ship.

'Another year has passed,' thought Crispus. 'Another Christmas with Gabe, now fourteen, with one more year on the *Intrepid* before Harvard.' Crispus had found a small pine and decorated it with a collection of shells he had gathered on his voyages. On a warm, winter day, bundled in heavy coats, the two of them spent a quiet hour watching the sea and harbor ships almost ice bound. They exchanged presents, a starfish for Gabe, a scarf knit by Gabe's mother for Tucks. They looked forward to spring, to warm afternoons when Gabe finished school, and time to talk again. They looked forward to better times, the end of soldiers in their city, and an open harbor ready for trade.

Crispus Attucks saw a healthier boy, stronger physically, but still agitated mentally, and prayed for full health to return to the child. 'Well, not a child anymore. In less than a year, Gabe would be fifteen and ready to work in his father's print shop over the summer, before departing for Harvard in the fall. Then there would be fewer afternoons together.'

Gabe saw a less happy friend. A friend perhaps too proud to ask for help from a print shop hurting from the lack of merchant ships as were other businesses. He also sensed anger just beneath the surface and worried that if times did not change, Crispus Attucks would join the mobs and crowds to harass the soldiers. Gabe worried about his friend. How he could be sure Tucks would be all right when he returned to school full time in the spring, and then spent the summer in Father's print shop.

The winter was a long one for Rafe. Too much time to read and not enough work to keep busy. He did not like what he read any more than he liked what he saw and heard. The soldiers were barely under control, and he could not really blame them. They were insulted, ignored, and literally left out in the cold. Any way they could, the people of Boston harassed the soldiers, charging more, delivering less, making them wait for necessary goods. The British ships in the harbor fared equally poorly. Sailors came to shore only in groups, and though impressment gangs no longer wandered about, a man had better be able to prove who he was when challenged by sentries looking for those who had jumped ship or deserted.

On the citizens' side, the 29th regiment seemed composed of the dregs, men who had a choice of hanging or joining the army. Even Thomas Hutchinson had been heard to say, "They are, in general, such bad fellows in that regiment, that it seems impossible to restrain them from firing upon an insult or provocation given them."

And, in fact, there had been an early scare. Now that British troops were here, supporters of the King had been sure that the leaders of the rebels would be charged and sent to London to be tried for treason. Wagers were even offered that Adams, Hancock, and Otis would hang. But, Adams and his friends had been careful, and no acts of treason could be proven against them. The supporters of the King felt betrayed, and the rebels felt energized.

Despite this reprieve, Faneuil Hall—the usual meeting place for citizens and their leaders, and for rabble rousing—was still in the hands of the British, who also over-ran the Town House where the legislature met. Guards challenged all who entered and left the town, and companies of soldiers patrolled near every ferry leaving for Boston. But the most threatening, it seemed to Rafe, was the main guard opposite the Boston Town House with cannon pointed at the door to the legislative chambers. One shot and all the city leaders would be gone.

On the other hand, Governor Bernard was leaving the colony. In many ways Rafe felt this was sad. Bernard's departure represented more than a change in government. Bernard had governed for five years of peace, a time when the colonists were truly attached to the King and to England. This all changed with the Stamp Act.

Rafe found it hard to support the English after this, and was each day becoming more and more a rebel. Rafe listened to Father, and read the exaggerations between the seemingly innocent lines. As he set type he read both sides of the issues, and while he agreed with the Whig, or rebel, position, he could see the "almost lies" they told against the Tories, the supporters of the King. Rafe had even read notes from Commodore Hood that said Bernard had "lost his way." If Bernard supported the colonists then the King would remove him. If he supported the King then the colonists would rebel. Bernard had walked a tightrope these last few years, and had, at last, fallen.

Rafe had almost felt pity for Bernard when he left, since his ship becalmed just outside the harbor, and the ex-governor would have been able to hear the bells and cannon celebrating his departure. Into the next day, still becalmed, Bernard would have seen the huge bonfires as the celebration continued.

'Poor Lady Bernard, what had she felt, left behind as her husband sailed away? I suppose all was forgiven, when the King created a Baronetcy for Bernard,' Rafe thought. 'There is so much pain, anger, bitterness: I fear what lies ahead. I fear the part my friends and I may yet play.'

And, as he set type to print Sam Adams' *Journal of Events*, he felt even more deeply the exaggerations. The *Journal* told of troops beating young boys in the streets, violating the Sabbath, carousing, and raping Boston matrons and young girls. It was published outside of Boston where no one could contradict what it claimed, nor did it explain that it was the mob violence which had caused the soldiers to be here in the first place. Rafe could only imagine what effect the *Journal* was having in the other colonies.

Rafe found it difficult to deny there were deep problems waiting to explode. In the summer of 1769, the British decided to remove two of the four regiments of British regulars from Boston. Sam Adams acted quickly and published a set of resolves which maintained that Parliament had no authority over the colony. Afraid of open rebellion until the House of Representatives voted down the resolves, the British halted the removal of the troops. When the town was quiet again, the troops were returned to Halifax. Rafe thought, 'Now what? The few troops left behind could be challenged, and probably defeated.'

1770

Jack Tar

Crispus Attucks reflected longingly on the time he had spent with young Gabe. Gabe baking in the sun and Tucks telling stories. He realized that his purpose had not just been to befriend a sickly boy but to tell someone his family's story. Gabe would remember, and though Tucks had no son, he had posterity in Gabe.

Gabe would not be pleased, but Crispus Attucks, a lowly Jack Tar, would no longer be a slave to the whims of the British. 'Jack Tar!' Tucks thought angrily. 'If we have to work in bad weather, the only way to keep a semblance of dryness is to cover our clothing with tar, and so we are identified by our clothing and not by the work we do. And now, soldiers are trying to take away the last employment available—the ropewalk. This was the last straw!' He remembered the afternoon he had explained to Gabe how a ropewalk worked. 'Gabe always wanted to know how things worked, and he would not settle for the short view. And the questions!'

"So, how does a ropewalk work? How can thee make heavy rope from so many little strands?"

Tucks patiently explained. "The work is done in long sheds, and the length of the finished rope is based on the length of the ropewalk. First, piles of fibers are spun into threads or yarns. The 'head' of hackled hemp is wrapped around the spinner's waist, and a loose end is made fast to a hook belted to the spinning wheel. As the wheel is turned by an assistant, the spinner moves backward down the ropewalk, feeding material from his waist and controlling the 'draw,' just as women do when they spin at

home. The two or three threads of yarn, usually from hemp grown here on our own farms, are twisted and formed into a strand. Three or more strands are twisted together to form a rope. To make very heavy cables, or hawsers, such as are attached to anchors, three or more ropes are laid together.

"The twisting has to be done in a straight line with the strands fully extended together. A twisting/spinning device at one end, a sledge to anchor the other end, and a grooved wedge called a top inserted among the strands and drawn ahead of the twist keeps the rope even and tight. The strands must be twisted evenly, without kinking, and all strands must be under equal tension until the whole process is finished. At each step, the direction of the twist is reversed, so the parts work against one another and keep the rope from untwisting. Finally the ends of the rope must be whipped off with crown-and-back-splices to keep them from unraveling."

In the end, Tucks had taken Gabe to the ropewalk to see the sight for himself.

In January of 1770, Sam Adams and a group of merchants met to plan ways to get reluctant merchants to follow the nonimportation plan. They decided on a boycott of the offenders and the publishing of their names. An additional consequence would be a constant harassment of those merchants.

In February, Sam Adams wrote the "Mysteries of Government," expressing all that Tucks felt about British rule. "Everyone knows that the exercise of the military power is forever dangerous to civil rights; and we have had recent instances of violence that have been offered to private subjects, and the last week, even to a magistrate in the execution of his office! Such violence is no more than might have been expected from military troops: A power, which is apt enough at all times to take a wanton lead, even when in the midst of civil society; but more especially so, when they are led to believe that they are become necessary to awe a spirit of rebellion, and preserve peace and good order."

"The idea that peace could come from force was not logical," Tucks said to himself.

Crispus Attucks liked Samuel Adams' statement of the rights of men and the rights of colonists as Englishmen.

Adams maintained the rights of "free course of justice in the courts of law, next to the right of petitioning the King and Parliament for redress of grievances, and lastly to the right of having and using arms for self-preservation and defense … These are the three great and primary rights of personal security, personal liberty and private property."

Crispus knew there would be no personal security or personal liberty if the British had their way. It seemed that only the worst sort of man became a British soldier. They were dirty and foul-mouthed. They were rude and had little education. They spent most of their free time drinking and fighting. They bothered civilians during the day and fought with them in taverns in the evening. It was true that they were given the same amount of disrespect that they gave others, but perhaps their most grievous fault was seeking the same casual labor that men like Tucks sought.

Crispus Attucks thought these soldiers represented the hearts of the officers he had shipped with, and the British heart was black—black as the darkness on a moonless night. All that had happened in his life, in his parents' lives, in his great-great-grandparents' lives was British caused. Left alone, the colonists tried to be fair. All slavery and Indian battles were caused by British political policies.

And, colonial rebellion, though well intentioned—like nonimportation—only made it harder on people like him. Ice in the harbor did not help the work situation either. No ships to unload or articles to sign. Crispus thought that while January and February were rough months for him, they were even harder on the poor and those with families to support.

Tucks thought all this competition for work would cause trouble. Fighting in the taverns was more frequent and more intense. Then Tucks felt the violence hit him in an unexpected way.

On February 22 of 1770, two young boys set up a sign identifying Theophilus Lillie as an importer, one of those merchants still importing from England. Lillie's friend and customs informer, Ebenezer Richardson, tried to destroy the sign, but the boys and a growing crowd prevented him from doing so. After some name calling by the boys and a crowd, Richardson headed home, but the growing crowd and the boys followed him and began yelling at Richardson and his wife.

The boys, now surrounded by the crowd, began throwing garbage at the Richardson home. Richardson was thoroughly angry and frightened at this time, a desperate combination. Richardson remembered the treatment of other customs officials: the public humiliation, the tarring and feathering, and he was not a brave man. He looked out from an upstairs window with a gun in his hand demanding that the crowd—yelling and throwing garbage—leave him alone. Instead of leaving, the boys and others began throwing anything they could find at the house. Surprising everyone, Richardson fired his gun. Sammy Gore was wounded, but Christopher Snyder was killed.

Christopher was only eleven years old, a few years younger than Gabe, and the same age as Gabe's young sister, Sarah. The fury that had been welling up in the heart of Crispus spilled over. That a child could be killed! That the child might have been Gabe—his posterity, his friend—was more than Crispus could stand. So, Tucks took part in the funeral along with thirteen hundred others. With each step, he saw the words on the head of the casket: "Innocence itself is no where safe."

There certainly would be no help from Governor Hutchinson. Hutchinson felt that poverty was good for people, it made them more industrious and more frugal. He had said after the funeral, "The boy that was killed was the son of a poor German. A grand funeral was, however, judged very proper for him."

Tucks thought, 'The son of a poor German, indeed. Did Governor Hutchinson have no sense of the people? Was it all right to kill a child— poor, German, or otherwise? That the boys threw garbage was no reason to shoot at them. Richardson could have fired into the air!'

Crispus vowed no other child would die. He would do all he could to get the black-hearted soldiers, customs officials, and their friends out of Boston. Even if he had to put his life on the line, Gabe and his family would be safe!

Posterity

G abe's parents were locked in conversation when Gabe came home for lunch. Mother spoke first, "Gabe, the weather will be fine soon, but I do not want thee to return to the *Intrepid*."

"Why, Mother? If it is about the boys, thee knows I would never behave as they did, or join a crowd. Besides that happened in town, the wharf is safe, especially with Tucks there."

Father said, "Gabe, it's not just the boys and what happened to them. Gregson's Wharf is not safe, not even with Crispus Attucks there. The angry mood of the whole town makes nowhere safe: The soldiers are angry at the way they have been treated, the citizens of Boston are angry about the Townsend Acts, and the men working the docks are worried about the soldiers taking the few available jobs. I want thee to come home directly from school and help thy mother, or help Rafe in the print shop."

"What about Tucks? How do I stay in contact with him?"

"First nice day, thee can go with Rafe and let him know what is going on. I am sure he will agree with me about the danger," said Father.

It was sunny, though cold, and Tucks was pacing the wharf. He did not want to miss Gabe if he came, and he did not want Gabe to stay on the docks. It was too dangerous, even if the *Intrepid* was far away from the ropewalk. The sky looked like it would storm later, so Tucks would make it an early day, if he could be sure Gabe was safe at home. He passed an old man several times in his pacing; he only noticed him because the old man reminded him of someone. The next time he passed, Tucks asked the old man how he was doing.

The old man said with a smile, "Why, Crispus, do not you remember your old friend?"

"Uncle? That be you? What you be doing here in Boston?"

"Same as you, I guess, lookin' for a berth. Did not expect the harbor to be iced over, or to see those warships aimed at the city. Must have been some interestin' times around here."

"Well, Uncle, I be not sure how interesting they be. I would have said dangerous, instead."

"Been lots of fights, have they? You been in any, boy?"

"No, you know me. Fighting be not what I be about, but lately I have been thinking that might be the way to go."

"You? Somethin' mighty big had to have happened for you to feel a fight comin' on."

"Yes. Wait a while; I have got to see that lad for a minute. You still be here?"

"Not sure where else I would go," replied Uncle.

"Gabe! Gabe! Wait up," Tucks called.

Gabe and Rafe had almost given up hope of finding Tucks, until they went around the back of the *Intrepid* and heard him calling. Gabe smiled at seeing Tucks and said, "Hey, Tucks! You remember my brother, Rafe?"

"Well, Rafael, it has been a time. You have grown since I saw you last. I heard you be quite a handy man in the print shop."

Rafe smiled. "Thanks, Tucks. It is what I seem meant to do. I sure like it better than school. Gabe here, he is the scholar in the family. Missed all that time and still is head of his class."

Gabe blushed, and then said hurriedly, "Tucks, I cannot come here anymore. But thee could come by the print shop and we can still be friends."

Tucks smiled. "Lad, we will always be friends, whether you come to the wharf or not. I have been pacing the wharf these last few days, hoping to see you to tell you not to come again. It is not safe, even here at the *Intrepid*. The docks are all in an uproar; the killing of the Snyder boy has everyone upset. Even me."

"Do not worry about me, Tucks. Thee knows I would not get

involved in the crowds. I did not even go to the funeral because Father thought there might be trouble. But there was not—I could have gone."

"There were lots of us there, lad, and there could have been trouble. I be just as glad you were not there. Hey, there is someone I want you to meet. See that old man over there?"

"Yes. Oh, Tucks, is that Uncle? Oh yes, I want to meet him. Rafe, Uncle is the one who taught Tucks all he knows about the sea. I want to meet him. I am sure Father will not mind."

"Thee go ahead, Gabe. I will wait here," Rafe said.

Tucks walked Gabe over to Uncle, introduced them, and left so Gabe could ask his usual million questions while he went back to talk with Rafe. "I am glad you came with him, Rafe."

"Father would not have let Gabe come alone. He said we live in dangerous times."

"Really dangerous if an eleven-year-old can get shot by a customs officer," Tucks said angrily.

"I have been reading about the work situation on the wharf. I do not understand why the soldiers have permission to work in their off hours," Rafe said quietly.

"I guess it is to keep them from drinking during the day, like they do all night," Tucks responded. "And, it is a lot of drinking they do. Even aboard ship, I have never seen a worse lot than this regiment. I do not think there be a man among them who can sign his name, or speak the King's English."

"Right! And Sam Adams has been sending petitions to Governor Hutchinson to have the troops removed. They feel there is a real tension between the town folk and the soldiers."

"Even more here, on the wharf. It is about all we can take to see those lobsterbacks steal every available job from us. We are stuck here. Ice on the harbor and warships aimed at the city. I do not see how violence can be avoided."

Rafe asked softly, "And thee, Tucks. Do thee see thyself in the violence? Thee seem so angry."

Crispus Attucks thought a moment and said firmly but quietly, "Sometimes a man has to act, even if it be against his principles. I have taken a lot from the British. I keep seeing Gabe in that coffin as it lowers into the ground. I have been careful what I say to him, Rafe, but I believe the time will come when we will all have to resort to violence, or give in and be slaves. I have served the British aboard ship; I do not intend to serve them on land too. I have read about taxes; I have seen and I do see customs officials; I have seen ships taken and ships burned. I have had all the British I can stand for a lifetime!" Tucks's anger grew stronger with each sentence; then he put on a calm face when he saw Gabe returning.

As he listened, Rafe thought, 'Father believes it is Sam Adams stirring up the crowds that causes so much violence. Father had said the death of the Snyder boy was bound to happen. Every customs official knew what angry crowds had done in the past. The fact that Richardson had a gun and used it was not surprising. Any animal that is forced into a corner will fight back. Father said he did not think Richardson really wanted to hurt either boy, but just fired.

'It was clear Sam Adams had not stirred up that crowd, it had just formed around the boys. Though Adams was making as much as he could over Snyder's death, he could not be held responsible for all of the violence. People could think for themselves, and not every mob would do more than throw some garbage. Here was Tucks, angry about all that had happened to him, and all that was happening to him. Sam Adams was not here telling Tucks what to think, Crispus Attucks could think for himself, and he was thinking violence.' Rafe was worried, and pleased that Gabe would not be on the wharf to see what might happen. Rafe's thoughts were interrupted by the return of his brother.

"What art thee thinking, Rafe?"

"Oh, nothing. Did thee have a nice talk with Uncle?"

"I sure did. He told me tales about Tucks that I had not heard before," Gabe answered. Then turning to his friend, "Tucks, I have to go now. Please stop by the print shop when thee can. I will be there in the afternoons."

Crispus Attucks looked lovingly at this boy who listened so much, and who understood him so well. "I will see you, lad. Looks like it be time to go anyway, it is starting to rain." After a quick hug Gabe and Rafe left.

"Michael, Michael Johnson."

Tucks had stepped inside a tavern for a quick drink. When he heard the name, he looked around, and then heard it called again. He thought, 'I have not been Michael Johnson for years.'

"Mike, Mike Johnson. Over here."

Tucks paid for his cider and then joined a group of young men looking at a broadsheet and arguing over its meaning.

"Davy?" Tucks asked.

The young man replied, "Yes! Mike, sit down. It's been a long time."

"What you be doing here?" Tucks asked his friend.

"Looking for a berth like everyone else. Say, what do you think this broadsheet is all about?"

Tucks read it, and then said with a twinkle in his eye, "I have seen these all over town. The British are warning people to be careful. You see, a number of their warships' crew have jumped ship." He paused, the young men getting the humor of this said, "No!"

"Yes, and a number of soldiers have deserted!"

Again the young men said, "No!"

Not smiling now, Tucks continued, "Here be the warning. There are British guards in town and on all the roads leading in or out of town, and guards on every ferry. The guards plan to capture the jumped crew and the deserters, so residents had better be able to prove who they are or they will be arrested."

Davy spoke, "I told you so. I knew Mike could explain it all." He nodded to the other young men at the table. After the young men shared their feelings about why anyone would want to jump ship or desert from a British anything, they ordered another round of drinks.

At this, Tucks stood up to leave. Davy offered to buy him another cider, but Tucks said, "Thanks. Another time. I want to head home before the weather gets worse."

As he walked away, one of the young men said, "He's a bit dark, your friend."

Another added, "A bit too uppity for such a dark man."

Davy responded angrily, "Yes, he's dark, but that six-foot giant can outwork anyone! He loves being aloft and can furl top gallants in a storm and not think twice. He also saved my life, and took the lashes for doing so. On one voyage we had a green captain and weak mates. If it had not been for Mike, we would have lost the mast in a storm. He got lashed that time for insubordination. He is a quiet man who does not spend his hard-earned money in taverns, like some fools I know, but if there is trouble I want that dark giant of a man on my side!"

At hearing Davy's defense of him, Tucks smiled to himself. He also overheard Patrick Carr and another Irishman talking. They were saying something about white boys and hedges, but Tucks didn't understand it as their Irish brogues were too thick.

When Tucks left the tavern to head home, Uncle was still on the wharf, now wearing his slicker in the rain. "Well, Uncle, what do you think of the lad?"

"He sure can ask the questions! And he sure loves you, boy."

"Where be you going to spend the night, Uncle?" Tucks asked.

"I guess right here," Uncle replied.

"No, you are not. Come on home with me. My cabin be clean and warm and you are welcome to what I have."

Uncle was more than pleased to go home with his friend. He could tell Crispus was troubled; the sailor had lost his sea calm and was fighting a storm on land.

The cabin they came to was plain. Outside logs, inside cold, though the fire was laid and quickly lit. As Uncle took off his slicker, Crispus hung it on a peg near the door, and then led the old man over to a chair before the fire. He placed a worn, but clean, afghan over Uncle's shoulders and a quilt over his knees, then set a covered pot on the fire. Soon the aroma of stew filled the room. When the stew was warmed, Crispus browned some bread over the fire. He ladled stew into round wooden bowls, broke the bread in hunks, and poured two cups of smuggled tea. Then, pulling up a bench to act as a table, Uncle and Crispus quietly enjoyed their meal. Crispus cleaned up the dishes and straightened the room then sat down to rest near the fire with Uncle.

For a while, neither one of them spoke; then Uncle said, "So, tell me what is goin' on, boy. It cannot just be these soldiers. I have seen you handle worse than that before."

"Yes, I know, Uncle. But it gets harder and harder to forgive and forget."

"It's that boy's death. Is not it?"

"Yes, I keep thinking of the lad, and Gabe, and my anger grows. I am afraid I will explode if I do not do something soon. If only I could get to sea, then I could get all my fight out in the rigging."

"Fightin' Nature ain't the same as fightin' a man. Furlin' sails in sleet like that poundin' against your window be dangerous business, but it be a business we know. Not this political business. But, from what you have said, Gabe will be safe. So, you can relax."

"You be right. Come, old man, let me get you to bed."

Tucks put Uncle into his own bed and then made a pallet for himself on the floor in front of the fire. As the wood turned into coals, Tucks lay awake, staring at the fire, at the coals, at nothing. He kept seeing the boy and the coffin lowered into the ground. He could hear the sound of shovels slicing into dirt, then the soft thud of soil hitting the wooden coffin. Over it all, he could hear the boy's father crying, "Son!"

Crispus Attucks dozed off before the coals became embers and awoke in time to add fuel to the embers for breakfast tea. The old man stirred. Tucks said, "Stay in bed until the room be warm. Here is a cup of tea. I will be off for a bit, but you are free to stay as long as you like. I would appreciate the company."

Lobsterbacks: You Do Not Dare Fire!

Uncle stayed and found work on the ropewalk. Sometimes Tucks joined him, but more often than not Tucks found work with a local merchant. On March 2, Uncle came home to tell Tucks about the trouble he had seen.

"Patrick Walker, an off-duty soldier, passed by John Gray's ropewalk looking for work. William Green, a worker on the ropewalk, told Walker to go clean an outhouse. Offended, the soldier began a fight with Green. Nicholas Ferriter, another sailor-worker, joined the fight. After Walker was knocked down, he left to get help. With his friend, Private William Warren, Walker gathered another eight soldiers, and returned within the hour to do battle. The soldiers were defeated again by the ropewalk sailors. The soldiers left and returned again, this time with forty in their number. Both sides went at each other with clubs and other weapons. Sam Gray, ropewalker and Irish immigrant, and Mat Killroy, a British soldier fresh from battling rebels in Ireland, fought each other with a vengeance, almost as though they had fought against each other, or someone like each other, before. The soldiers were defeated."

Tucks was angry. Not only did he worry about Gabe, but now Uncle could get hurt. Tucks decided to leave the better-paying job with the merchants to work on the ropewalk with Uncle, at least until all of this trouble blew over.

In the morning, the fighting resumed and continued over the next two days. When Tucks's back was turned, Uncle was shoved down and told to go home to his grandchildren and let a man have work. On the other side of the fight, Private John Rodgers had both his arms and skull fractured. The soldiers said they would have their revenge.

As Tucks observed Uncle over those days, he saw a man growing more and more frail. Even ropewalk work was too much for him. When the soldier shoved Uncle, Tucks was not sure Uncle could get up. With each passing day, Crispus Attucks grew angrier and angrier. There was no chance of sea for him with an iced-over harbor and British ships. Few merchant ships would risk entering the harbor for fear their crew would be impressed. And, if Uncle could get to sea, he would never return, that much was certain.

What future was there for Tucks? He thought, 'None. I can get old and die at sea like Uncle might or I can fight like the others to protect my work on land. Is there not something more? When will we ever be free of the British?'

When the soldiers came back to the ropewalk for the third day, Crispus was ready. Armed with a cudgel, he struck those who attacked his friends and any who threatened Uncle. Afterward, Crispus had mixed feelings. He could fight, but there was no joy in it. The British soldiers had to know the colonists would fight for work and for the ability to make a living, before they would become slaves to British whim.

The evening of March 5, 1770, was chilly. There was still snow on the ground and a weak light from a quarter moon. A lone sentry, Private Hugh White, stood guard before the Customs House on King Street. As Captain Goldfinch was passing, a young shop apprentice, Edward Garrick, began harassing Goldfinch for not paying his bill. The Captain, a receipt in his pocket, ignored Garrick. Private White, who could not stand to see his captain harassed, spoke up and told the boy that Goldfinch always paid his bills.

Finishing a glass of cider with Davy and his young friends in Samuel Wetherold's Tavern, on the corner of Kilby and King Streets, Crispus Attucks heard that a lad had been struck with a musket for daring to say bills were not being paid. It seemed to Tucks, or Michael Johnson as Davy called him, like a repeat of the Snyder incident. Tucks thought, 'What is it with the British and their killing of children?' The list ran through his head: 'Red, the attacks on Davy, Christopher Snyder, and

now this new boy.' Tucks grabbed a club and took off running down
King Street, followed by a group of thirty sailors. He vowed to stop the
killing, and to teach this soldier a lesson he'd never forget. The others
who followed Tucks were looking for another fight with the soldiers, soldiers who had taken their jobs and starved their families. For some, the
fight was against soldiers who had attacked their way of life in Ireland,
forcing them to leave home and family or end up in a British prison, and
who now were beginning their destruction of another homeland. By now
the bells were pealing like there was a fire and crowds gathered around
Private White who had struck the Garrick boy.

Crispus Attucks shouldered his way to the front of the crowd, just as Captain Preston and his men arrived to help Private White. Tucks couldn't believe the soldiers the captain had brought with him. It was as though this captain wanted trouble, and Tucks was willing to oblige him. Among the men Captain Preston had chosen to rescue White, were Privates Killroy, Montgomery, and Warren. Tucks recognized Warren and Killroy from the fights at the ropewalk. He thought Killroy had been the one to knock down Uncle, but he could not be sure. A larger crowd had followed the soldiers to King Street.

The soldiers formed a semi-circle, with their guns loaded and bayonets forward. Captain Preston stood in front of his troops and pleaded for peace, but the crowd pushed forward saying, "Damn your bloods. Why do not you fire?"

Angered at the bayonets, Crispus knocked a gun out of one of the soldier's hands. Then he grabbed at Warren's weapon. He seized it. In the shoving confusion, Private Warren was able to grab it back. At the same time, someone threw a club that knocked down Private Montgomery. When he rose, Montgomery pulled the trigger. After a short pause Killroy fired his weapon, and then other soldiers shot into the crowd.

Crispus Attucks fell, thinking, 'Freedom. Dearest Lord, dearest Gabe, at last I am free ...'

Gabe could not sleep. It seemed the fire bells had rung all night. There was shouting in the streets and he heard gunfire. It was after midnight before Gabe finally slept.

Father let his children sleep. There would be no school today, and maybe not for some time. At any rate, none of his children would leave home today. He had even closed the print shop and locked the shutters, not knowing what the crowds might do after the craziness of last night.

Father had tried to explain to his sons, after the Snyder boy's death, how this violence could have been prevented. He believed if the colonists had obeyed the various attempts by the British to raise taxes, and only protested through petition, then the customs officials would not have been badly treated, and would not be frightened. There would be no soldiers in town, and no British warships in the harbor, and no frightened Richardson shooting into the crowd to save himself.

Father knew Rafe might understand how this awful death of Crispus Attucks could have been prevented. There would have been no soldiers taking work, or drinking in taverns, or harassing civilians, and hence no Captain Goldfinch to protect, no Garrick collecting bills, no ringing bells, and no blood in the streets.

But Gabe would only know his friend was dead. And this death might put Gabe over the edge. He had been doing so well, even accepting the necessity of parting with Crispus Attucks. Tucks had visited the print shop only twice in the two weeks since they had to part. He came just enough to keep Gabe calm and not enough to be a bother. Tucks always seemed reasonable and calm, so Father could not understand how or why Crispus Attucks had let himself be caught up in last night's foolishness.

Gabe slept until noon. He awoke refreshed and had forgotten the night's disruptions. He did not seem to notice the forced smiles, or that Father and Rafe were in the sitting room instead of in the print shop. Sarah had been home from school with a cold for several days, so seeing her was expected. Gabe said, "I know I missed school, but I really enjoyed sleeping in. I feel great!" It was then he noticed the solemn faces, and said, "What happened? Was there a bad fire last night?"

"No, Gabe. No fire. There was more violence," Father said.

"The soldiers and dock workers again?" Gabe asked Rafe.

Rafe looked at Father and said, "Yes. It seemed they had taken a day off for Sunday, but decided to finish the fight on Monday. So ..." Father nodded for Rafe to continue. "So, people and soldiers were out looking for each other. Neither side was in the right. Someone told Ensign Gilbert Carter that the inhabitants of Boston would not leave any soldier alive in Boston. Soldiers, on the other hand, threatened to knock down any inhabitant they could lay their hands on. Each side spread rumors and each side was ready to continue the fight they had begun last week at the ropewalk. They fought again last night."

Father picked up the story from there, "In order to prevent more fighting, John Gray, the ropewalk owner, and Lieutenant Colonel Dalrymple, the commanding military officer in Boston, decided to do what they could to settle people down. Gray fired Green—who had insulted Private Warren—and Dalrymple told his soldiers not to leave the barracks unless they were in large groups and to avoid the ropewalk. But on Monday, the soldiers posted a handwritten notice:

Boston Marcy ye 5th 1770

This is to Inform ye Rebellious People in Boston that ye Soldeirs in ye 14th and 29th Regiments are Determend to Joine to Gether and Defend them Selves against all Who shall Oppose them

Signed ye Soljers of ye 14th & 29th Regiments

"During the day, Gabe, there were several fights in different parts of town and people seemed to enjoy spreading rumors, on both sides. Robert Pierpoint said soldiers were murdering inhabitants, and so he hit a corporal for having a bayonet in his hand. Other incidents occurred, both at the south end and the north end of Boston. From there, crowds began to converge on the town center. There was a battle about 9:00 p.m. in Boylston's Alley, where groups of soldiers were going around the area crying, 'Where are your sons of liberty? Where are the damned boogers, cowards, where are your liberty boys?'

"On Cornhill, residents were caught and harassed by soldiers as they tried to enter their homes. Sailors and dock workers coming from the harbor were attacked and fought back against the soldiers."

Gabe interrupted, "Tucks! Was Crispus Attucks in that group?"

Father wanted Gabe to know the whole story before he answered, "We do not know. What we do know is that a crowd went to the gates of Murray's barracks and there were arguments back and forth. One soldier kept coming out with a rifle, ready to shoot into the crowd. He had to be sent inside twice before he could be kept inside. So, when the action there ended, and when the town bells began to ring, most of the crowd went to the Main Guard at the Town House. Then, as there were even more bells ringing, a large crowd gathered to attack the Main Guard and to get the soldiers out of Boston. On guard duty was Private White.

"Some boys from the crowd told the story of what Private White had done. Young Garrick was harassing Captain Goldfinch for not paying his bills. Angered by the treatment of a British officer, Private White struck Garrick with his musket. Young Garrick explained to several people what had happened to him, and a crowd gathered. Hearing of the large crowd gathered at King Street, Captain Preston and some soldiers came to the aid of Private White. Some ice and snowballs were thrown by the crowd, also coal and clubs. One soldier was knocked down, and when he got up, he fired—whether by accident or on purpose, we don't know—and then, other soldiers fired. Four men were killed and eight wounded. While the crowd helped the wounded, the soldiers were able to slip away. Governor Hutchinson arrived and got people to settle down and go home."

"What a horrible night, Father. Do we know yet who was hurt?" Gabe asked.

Father said quietly, "Yes. Sam Adams came by this morning with a broadsheet to print, containing the names of those injured. Patrick Carr was wounded severely, also wounded were Christopher Monk, John Clark, Edward Payne, John Green, Robert Patterson, David Parker, and Benjamin Burdick, Jr." Pausing for a moment, Father reluctantly continued, "And, several were killed: Samuel Gray, James Caldwell, Samuel Maverick, and, I am so sorry to say, your Crispus Attucks."

"My Tucks? Father, no!" Gabe screamed. Then he fainted.

Gabe was feverish for two days; tossing and turning in half sleep filled with nightmares that he did not awaken from. Dr. Warren called several times to see Gabe. "Gabe's mind battles for control of his heart," he said. "In time, he will be himself again. It is important to watch him, even after he recovers. His mind is still weak from his long illness and another shock could set him back. Each shock may gain in severity, and at some point, his mind might not return. It is vital to keep his mind as calm as possible."

Gabe did come back to them after his feverish time, though weak and listless. He did not seem to care about drawing, or writing, or his studies. He lay in the window seat and looked out to the harbor. It was Rafe who first remembered Uncle, and that he might be in need. After much discussion, for nothing was known of this "uncle," Mother agreed that if Rafe went along, Gabe looking for Uncle might be a good idea.

So, one sunny day, Father released Rafe from the print shop. Rafe went to Gabe and said, "I was thinking Gabe ..."

"If thee are here to tell me it's time to forget Tucks, just go away."

"No, Gabe. I do not think you should forget Tucks. I am here because I was wondering about Uncle. Without Tucks to care for him, I wonder how he is getting along. It has been over a week since Tucks died. When I spoke to Father, he suggested it might be a good idea to check on Uncle and to see if he needs anything. I thought thee might like to go along, if thee feel up to a walk."

"Sorry, Rafe," Gabe said, brightening, "Yes, I would like to go. Thee might not recognize him without me."

Uncle

The boys headed first to the ropewalk, where they were told Uncle had not been seen for some time. Next they checked the wharf where they had first met him, but he had not been there. It was Gabe who suggested that if Uncle were ill he would be at Tuck's cabin. Rafe asked, "Do thee know where it is?"

Gabe replied, "I am not sure. We could we ask someone." They headed over to the harbor bank where the poor had their cabins. They saw Mary Watson hanging out laundry. She pointed out the small cabin. She said she had thought about checking on the old man but had not had time. She was worried because it was still chilly and there was no smoke coming from the chimney.

Rafe and Gabe hurried to the log cabin. They knocked but there was no answer. The door was unlocked so they opened it and looked in. The cabin was cold but neat. The box next to the fireplace was stocked with wood, a pallet neatly rolled against one wall, and the rough-hewn table was clean with two washed wooden bowls stacked with spoons near a lidded pot. In the far corner was a bed. Under two quilts they found a gray-haired and very pale Uncle. Uncle raised his head and said faintly, "I thought you boys might come."

Rafe quickly lit a fire. Gabe brought Uncle a cup of water and held him up so he could drink. Uncle said his thanks then lay back down. Gabe and Rafe looked at each other and thought how lucky they were that Rafe remembered Uncle. A few more days and they might have found only a cold memory of this friend of Crispus Attucks.

Between the light from the window and the light from the fire, the boys could see the cabin clearly. Everything was handmade, roughly hewn from logs or from wood tossed upon the harbor banks from the sea. In the far corner was the bed, and next to it were two shelves where a Bible and some papers were neatly stacked, underneath the shelves stood Tuck's sea chest holding a candle and matches. At the end of the bed was another sea chest, probably Uncle's. In the center of one wall was a fireplace of neatly mortared stones, taken from the harbor shore line. In front of the fireplace were two chairs, and a worn rag-rug between them and the fire. In the center of the room stood a bench and a newly made small table. On the opposite wall were more shelves, one wider than the others held bowls and pots. The fourth wall was empty, but the dirt floor was hardened and neatly swept.

This was a different view of Crispus Attucks the homemaker. A man who lived alone and spent time whittling bowls, gathering driftwood, cutting and shaping trees to make chairs and tables, benches and a bed. When Gabe had seen Tucks the second time, he was neat and trim, his mending done carefully. Gabe had never thought about what that might mean, but now he had a glimpse of the orderly man his friend really was. 'How does such an organized man get caught up in crowds? And killed?' wondered Gabe.

As the room warmed, Uncle said he thought he would like to get up and sit next to the fire. Rafe and Gabe helped him, put a quilt across his lap, and a worn afghan across his shoulders. Uncle spoke. "This is just like my first night with Crispus." A single tear trickled down his lined cheek. "You cannot imagine how good he was to me, and what a friend. He was a real hero, you know!"

"Yes, we know. He finally fought against his will for freedom's sake."

"Well, yes. That too. I will bet he never told you the real stories about when he was a hero."

Gabe said, "He told me some stories. But he never spoke of being a friend, only that thee were a friend to him. And he never said he was a hero."

"Put another log on that fire, will you Rafe, and I will tell you a story. He must have told you about our first meetin'."

The boys nodded.

"Well, I had never seen a man so green. When he went up the ropes to the mast, I thought he would lose it, but he did not. I have never seen anyone learn so fast. He seemed to know what to do to furl those sails and lash them down. Climbing down was the hardest, the ship was still rockin' from side to side, but no longer in danger of tippin'. So, the danger passed and Tucks came down the mast lookin' down. That never be a good idea. He froze for an instant, and then resumed climbin'. I said he had done good work for a landsman, only to watch him get sick over the side.

"It was a good, sturdy little sloop; our captain worked as one of us and made the voyage a pleasant one. Our wages were ready at the end, and Tucks and I quickly signed articles on the next merchant ship to leave. Like I said, he learned quickly everythin' I knew, and he was always watchin' the mates and captain to see what they did, even askin' questions. I remember one captain sayin', 'Tucks, if you were not such an able seaman, I would not stand here answerin' you.' That was a real compliment, for a captain to answer a seaman's questions. In those days it was 'fresh winds' all the time, the sailin' easy, as were the captains and crews we worked with.

"We became separated after a time. Crispus tried whalin', and then the larger merchant ships. Years later, we happened to sign articles on another ship together, but there was no questionin' on this one. I had never seen such a captain in all my time at sea. He was a sadistic monster, hated swearin', and carried a club with him all the time. If he heard you swear, he hit you over the head. He hit one man so hard it broke his skull and we could see his brains. The sailor was quickly sewn in his hammock and slid overboard without anyone sayin' a word over him. Tucks and I were the only two who witnessed this beatin', so the captain and first mate kept a close eye on us to see if we would tell others. We did not, then.

"On that same voyage, was a kid called Red, because of his red hair and freckles. For some reason the captain singled Red out for 'special treatment.' Each time he passed Red, the captain would give him a 'love tap.' Often Red would finish his watch with a bloody nose or a lump on his skull. Crispus took a likin' to Red, only a kid about fourteen, and taught him how to splice rope and mend sail. Red seemed all fingers and his stitches were uneven. The captain walked by one day and saw the work Red was doin' and hit him a good one on the shoulder. The blow shoved his shoulder out of joint, and it took the surgeon, and Tucks, and me to force it back into place. After that, Red said he did not figure he would live to see the end of the voyage.

"Well, we got someone to trade watches with Red and he became part of our mess. Most of the time the captain slept durin' our watch, but some days he was on deck. (You know, the dog watch is two hours, so each mess rotates the time of day they are on duty.) We did our best to protect Red, but with storms and other duties we could lose track of him. The captain always seemed to know when Red was unprotected and the beatings continued. Once I remember he was beaten black and blue on his arms, legs, back, and chest. We did not think he would make it, but he was a tough kid and went back to work on the next watch. Not that the captain would have let him rest.

"Once a couple of sailors were late gettin' back from shore leave and the captain had another punishment up his sleeve. I have heard it called 'whip and pickle.' Whatever you call it, the punishment did not fit the crime. The two sailors were tied legs and arms apart from their body. Each was given forty lashes with a cat-o-nine-tails. Then the brine from the salt pork was poured over their cuts. The salt in the sliced flesh was more painful than the lashin' itself. And, since it came from the salt pork, the brine made the cuts more likely to fester.

"As the voyage continued, the captain grew more irrational and the punishments grew more severe. Men who were whipped and pickled, were whipped and pickled two or three times, one right after the other, and the lashin's were more than doubled. One sailor who protested, was lashed, pickled, and then tied to the topmast for a day without food or water. About this time, the captain decided we were all shirkers and cut the food and beer rations first by a third, then by half. Some of us old timers taught the youngsters how to fish, but after a time the captain confiscated all the fishin' gear saying our rations were enough, and if we had time to fish we had time to do more work. He wanted the ship sparklin'!

"Red grew weaker as time went by. We all did of course, but we were not gettin' beaten several times a week. When Red fell from the topmast into the sea, the captain said we did not have time to rescue him. I watched for Red, he only came to the surface once, looked at me, and then sank out of sight. Crispus must have seen what I did for he told me he would never let another boy be hurt.

"When the captain turned his attention to young Davy, now that Red was gone, Tucks waited until the captain was alone to speak to him. I do not know what Crispus said, but the next day Tucks was accused of shirkin' his work and lashed forty times. There was no picklin' or tying to the topmast. But the captain left that boy alone and chose grown men for his sadistic games. I know in my heart that Crispus took the lashin' for speaking up.

"That was not the first time, nor the last time when Crispus stood up for someone. Sometimes he was punished instead, other times a rational captain would hear Tucks out, for Tucks was not a sailor who ever threatened or caused trouble, but was always reasonable. And that was unusual behavior amongst seamen. Their work was hard and dangerous, so often a crew would sign a round-robin against a troublesome captain. A round-robin was a warnin' and not quite mutiny. A rational captain would listen, a fearful captain would listen, and an angry captain would listen. For, if the captain did not listen, mutiny would follow."

Gabe asked, "Could not the captain just punish the ones who signed the round-robin?"

"Well, Gabe, it would depend on how many of the crew signed. Usually by that time, the crew would mostly be of one mind. They would draw two circles. In the inner circle they would state their grievances. Then, on the outer circle, they would sign their names. They would begin at the four compass points, then fill in the areas in between. Each signature would cross the outer circle so no one could tell who signed first."

"Is not there any way to prevent sadistic captains?" Gabe asked.

Uncle replied, "There is the Admiralty Court that hears cases sailors bring. But it can be expensive. Usually sailors just tell other sailors not to ship with a particular captain, but if you are pressed, or have no other opportunity available, you might sign articles hopin' for the best." Uncle paused, coughed, and then said, "I am sorry, boys, but I need to rest now. Will you come back?"

Rafe said, "I am sure Father will let us. Do thee need anything before we go? Can we bring thee anything?"

Uncle said, "I have soup and bread, and Mrs. Watson said she would stop by later with some stew. I think I will be right in a day or so and ready to work again. But I sure would love some company."

Gabe said softly, "And I would like to come back and hear more."

The boys left, making sure there was enough wood cut and in the wood box.

Rafe was right. Father said, "Of course, thee may return. Mother will even send some of her vegetable soup, and maybe some apples or fresh biscuits."

Mother said, "I will be sure to have a treat ready for tomorrow afternoon! I am so proud of thee, caring for the old man. I am sure Tucks would be proud of thee too. Now, Gabe, I want thee to rest before supper. Thee hast walked far."

Gabe was still weak and all of a sudden felt his exhaustion, so much so that he did not complain about the nap or being treated like a sick child. Rafe and Father went back to the print shop to finish the day's work. Rafe told his father that Uncle needed them, and looked quite ill. But, that Gabe needed Uncle perhaps more than he was needed. Rafe said Gabe came alive again listening to the old man's stories.

That evening, two important events happened. First, Gabe wrote all that Uncle had told him in his journal before he went to bed that evening. Second, Sam Adams stopped by the print shop with his next tirade against the soldiers and the horror of the massacre, and with news. John Adams, his cousin and lawyer, would be defending the soldiers in their trial. Father thought how lucky it was Gabe was asleep already and didn't hear that a cousin of Sam's had taken the soldier's side in the trial.

The next day, Gabe felt strong enough to go to school; especially since they were to see Uncle that afternoon. Gabe arrived home feverish again and ranting. "They have put off the trial until October, and John Adams is going to defend those murderers. How is that possible? Isn't he Sam Adams' cousin? Have you seen the Revere print? It shows those murderers firing right into the crowd. How can anyone defend them? They should be hung; they do not deserve a trial."

Father interrupted. "That is hardly the voice of a son of mine. Do thee not believe in the law? Do thee not believe in justice? What do thee think would happen if those soldiers were just hung without a trial? What would that tell the British about Boston's justice and equality? Is justice only for the people we like? Do thee really think Mr. Adams is taking the case because he believes in the soldiers' actions? Do thee not think this decision required much thought? And, do thee think John Adams would have made this choice without the encouragement of Sam Adams? This is an important trial, it will show the King and others the nature of our character. Remember, violence begets violence. The British would be here with five regiments to restore order if the soldiers were hung without a trial. And, while thee art working thyself up to be ill again, there is poor old Uncle waiting for supper. Do not forget thy responsibilities in thy grieving, Gabe. Do not forget thy promises and duty to others, especially thy duty to Uncle."

A properly chastened Gabe hung his head. "Thee art right, Father. I need to control my anger, especially when others are depending on me. I will get what Mother has prepared and come back to get Rafe."

After Gabe left the print shop, Father said to Rafe, "Thee keep careful watch on him. He is in no shape to leave home, but seeing Uncle will probably do him good. Come back early if thee can."

Rafe said, "Yes, Father. I have seen Gabe like this before and I worry about him. I hope visiting Uncle will calm him."

The visits did keep Gabe calm. Being with Uncle was almost like being with Tucks. At the very least, there was a kinship with Uncle, a person with whom Gabe could share his thoughts and feelings, a person who could understand because Uncle had loved Tucks as Gabe had loved him. Gabe had a new worry though: Uncle didn't seem to be getting better despite the warm food and the visits.

One afternoon, the boys arrived at Tucks's cabin to find Uncle in bed. The fire was low, but not out, and Rafe had little trouble stirring it into flame. As Rafe added more wood, Gabe gave Uncle a drink of water and, at Uncle's request, helped him into a chair in front of the fire. Gabe covered the old man with a quilt and afghan as before, then filled the kettle with water for smuggled tea while Rafe set Mother's soup on to heat.

Uncle seemed wan and weaker than before. When the boys told Uncle he did not need to talk, he said he did. "You have to hear this because I do not think I will be here when you come again. I have been sailin' on an ash breeze for several days now, just pullin' my boat along, and my oars be ready for a long rest, as be my mind." He paused for a moment. "I want you to know that Crispus Attucks's mother made these quilts, the afghan, and the rag-rug. He would want you to know they are special." Uncle stopped and took a sip of tea. "Crispus Attucks would want you to know he did what he did for you boys, for me, and for all seamen. He was not a person always ready to fight, but he could fight when he saw no other way out. He had changed, he told me, after the British warship impressment. The captain was brutal, the discipline harsh, and any infraction met with the lash or worse. The hardest part for Crispus was the stupidity of the captain. Tucks said he made the mistake of pointin' out an error, and though his intervention saved the ship, he was severely lashed."

"He only told me others were lashed," Gabe said.

"He did not want you to worry. But most of all, he did not want either of you boys to go to sea. The sea gave Crispus freedom from one kind of slavery only to put him in another kind of slavery. He knew he had no more future than I have. He would not let the British keep you and your family under their sadistic thumb, and so fought when he had to."

"But why did he use the name Michael Johnson? Everyone thought at first it was Michael who was killed, not Tucks."

"I am not sure, Gabe. But I think he used that name to say he was free. You must know he could not use his real name the first few years he signed articles as a sailor. So, he used a free name. And, who would follow a slave or an Indian? Men would only follow a free man, so that night he declared himself truly free. And they did follow him, he was not alone that night. Oh, I do not mean the rest of the crowd. Crispus Attucks led a group of sailors. They had all had their fill: the boy's death, the lack of employment, and the fights at the ropewalk. I guess even my gettin' hit on the head added to his anger. It is true that Sam Adams and others visited the docks remindin' sailors and dock workers what the British soldiers had done, what their occupation meant here in Boston. But all Adams did was reinforce what the men were feelin'. Crispus Attucks, your Tucks, was really a hero. He fought for all of us, the seamen, the poor, the slave, the Indian. He fought for all of us to have a better life. He loved his vision of what this country could be, not what it is. He especially loved you and your 'peculiar people' as he called your family and church." Uncle coughed long and hard, and stopped talking. He was able to eat a little soup and a biscuit, and then asked to be helped back to bed. He said, "I will not be here tomorrow. Do not bother coming."

That night, Gabe again wrote in his journal all that Uncle had said, and all that he was thinking and feeling. Uncle seemed to understand the world and Gabe needed to understand. The boys went to visit the next afternoon, but all they found was a neatly made bed, a clean cabin, and an empty spot where Uncle's sea chest had sat at the end of the bed. No one seemed to know what happened to Uncle, he was just gone. A small sloop had left the harbor, but how Uncle could have signed aboard, much less carried his sea chest was more than anyone could figure out.

Gabe was quiet when he returned home. He went right to his window seat and quickly fell asleep. Rafe returned to the print shop and told Father what they had discovered. Father asked how Gabe was doing, and Rafe said he came home and went right to sleep. Rafe said that he worried about Gabe. "What will happen now that Uncle is gone?"

Father said, "I do not know. I am worried too."

The Rift

For the next few days, Gabe was quiet. He went to school and came home without speaking. He napped before supper, or brought Mother water, but said nothing. One evening, Father decided to speak.

"Son, I think it's time to talk. The soldiers are gone now. I know thee learned Patrick Carr died today, so it's over. It's time to go on. Thee hast heard the reasons for John Adams representing the men. Thee knows why Crispus Attucks did what he did. Thee knows the truth of what happened. Use thy great powers of reason and come back to us. Thee knows that violence breeds violence. Thee also knows that sometimes before the next round of violence there is a step of good. Remember the good Crispus Attucks died for."

Gabe reluctantly looked up at his father. "I know all that, but I mourn the loss of my friend. There is a part of me that's angry that he acted as he did and left me behind. No, Father, I do not mean I would have gone with Michael Johnson. I mean I am angry he left me. That he made the choice for violence instead of me. Oh, I do not know what I mean. I am angry. I am sad. I feel more alone than I have for a long time. Even when Tucks was away at sea, I always knew that one day I would go to the *Intrepid* and there he would be. What do I do, Father? How do I get rid of the pain?"

Father replied softly, "The pain will get less but will always be a part of thee. Why do not thee say everything thee are feeling in thy journal? Later thee can go back and re-read it when thee feels less pain."

And so, Gabe did. He wrote all that Uncle had told him and what those words had meant to him. He wrote of his loss of Tucks, his anger, his sadness. He wrote of losing Uncle, who had given Gabe an insight into the part of Crispus Attucks he did not know. He wrote of the soldiers leaving Boston and Patrick Carr dying. And he wrote of Father who could not understand, and Rafe who did.

For Gabe, several things seemed very clear this sad summer of 1770. First, he must finish school so that he could be prepared for Harvard. School was vital if he were to make a difference in this new country—for Gabe no longer thought of Massachusetts as a colony but as a part of a larger country consisting of all colonies on this side of the Atlantic Ocean. Next, with Rafe's help, for Rafe could be less emotional than Gabe, he needed to understand all that Crispus Attucks was, not just the friend he knew. Finally, there had to be a way to act against the British. Not so much for vengeance but as a way to fight back without violence. Gabe felt this was his calling, to ensure that no other Crispus Attucks would have to be placed in such a British box that he must die to survive.

Throughout the long spring and longer summer, Gabe studied, worked, and thought. The trial, the massacre trial, the soldier's trial, lay ahead, and justice lay ahead, and perhaps the truth lay ahead; though neither Rafe nor Gabe really believed the truth would win. The brothers had talked often about that horrible night and Crispus.

From what Patrick Carr had said, the soldiers had been in real danger, and Captain Preston had tried to calm the crowd and the soldiers. At one point, Preston had even stood between the soldiers and the crowd to prevent violence. But violence had happened anyway. In their hearts, Rafe and Gabe believed it was all Walker, Warren, Green, and Sam Gray who began the fight over work and the lack of it. Preston had simply brought the wrong men to solve the problem. The dock workers recognized the men they had fought before and were ready to fight them again. The first shot was probably the gut reaction of an angry man not a thinking soldier. The later shots were fired by frightened men who perhaps thought the order to fire had been given.

Luckily Preston had been able to quiet his men, and the crowd, surprised by bloodshed, had not acted immediately, so the soldiers could escape and find safety. The soldiers were murderers, just as Gabe had said that day he returned home from school. But the killing was an accident. A horrible accident committed by men out of control and angry and frightened British soldiers, who had been beaten by common dock workers the week before.

Where Father was wrong, the boys believed, was that it was the

British not the colonists who had caused all this violence. If the British had recognized the efforts the colonists had made in fighting the French and Indian War, if the British had asked for help in reducing the debt, then none of this would have happened. The colonists would have felt part of England, loyal to the mother country, not put upon by a government in which they had no say. There would have been no mobs, no violence, no customs officials causing trouble, and no need for troops or warships in the harbor. In fact, even if England had not asked the colonies for money, they would still be money ahead by not having to pay for customs officials, troops, and warships. All this reaction had to be expensive. And now, after the soldiers fired on civilians, who wanted to be part of a mother country that punished her children by killing them?

And the boys—especially Gabe—wondered who this friend Tucks was. Crispus Attucks, the slave, the Indian, the able seaman, or violent Michael Johnson, the cudgel carrying leader of mobs? In his heart Gabe knew Tucks was both. It would not have been possible for Tucks to have been the gentle man he was with Gabe and have survived as a seaman. Rafe had told Gabe what he knew of sailors, how they went on strike, or mutinied, or became pirates. These seemed to be their only defense against a system that earned its living on their backs, and then did its best to cut rations, over charge them for supplies, or in some other way cheat them of the salary they earned. That Tucks had a cabin meant he had not spent all his time drinking and fighting, but that he knew how to use a cudgel meant he had experience with brawls.

It was Crispus Attucks's mother's influence, perhaps, that had brought on the gentleness, the affection and appreciation for God and His creation. And, perhaps slavery gave Tucks an appreciation of the times aloft, and the humility to work hard. Gabe wondered too if Uncle's presence and the buildup of anger had made Tucks eager to act when the time came. Tucks had said Gabe was his posterity. Tucks had told Gabe his life story. Maybe Crispus Attucks did not believe he would have a long life or a life worth living if the British had their way.

Rafe said he believed that Gabe's reasoning worked except for the last bit about a life not worth living. Rafe said whatever the real reason, when Tucks as Michael Johnson led the sailors to King Street, it probably had more to do with work and the ropewalk fighting than to do with life and death.

Gabe decided Rafe was probably right. So, Gabe studied to prepare for Harvard College and waited for the October trial, after making Rafe promise that when the time was right they would take action.

October 1770

The Trial

The trial had several parts. First was the hearing to see if Captain Preston had given the order to fire. Many of the more radical patriots were sure that was true. Gabe and Rafe did not believe the Adams' propaganda, as it did not seem reasonable for Preston to have so ordered.

On March 12, 1770, *The Boston Gazette* and *Country Journal* maintained that:

> "Captain Preston with a party of men with charged bayonets came from the main guard to the commissioner's house, the soldiers pushing their bayonets, crying, 'make way!' They took place by the custom house and, continuing to push to drive the people off pricked some in several places, on which they were clamorous and, it is said, threw snowballs. On this, the Captain commanded them to fire; and more snow balls coming, he again said, 'Damn you, fire, be the consequence what it will!'
>
> "One soldier then fired, and a townsman with a cudgel struck him over the hands with such force that he dropped his firelock; and, rushing forward, aimed a blow at the Captain's head which grazed his hat and fell pretty heavily upon his arm. However, the soldiers continued the fire successively till seven or eight, or as some say, eleven guns were discharged. By this fatal maneuver three men were laid dead on the spot and two more struggling for life; but what showed a degree of cruelty unknown to British troops, at least since the house of Hanover has directed their

operation, was an attempt to fire upon or push with their bayonets the persons who undertook to remove the slain and wounded …

"Tuesday morning presented a most shocking scene, the blood of our fellow citizens running like water through King Street and the Merchant Exchange, the principal spot of the military parade for about eighteen months past. Our blood might also be tracked up to the head of Long Lane, and through divers other streets and passages."

After reading the article, Rafe explained to Gabe, "The troops had probably had their bayonets at the ready, but if anyone was pricked it was because they got too close. The troops had not fired on those trying to remove the slain and wounded, Preston prevented it, and then the soldiers were too busy getting out of there. And as for blood running like water in the streets, there was snow on the ground. If the blood left a spot other than on King Street it was because someone tracked it there on their boots. Both boys agreed that Sam Adams had been able to use his propaganda techniques to get the troops removed and put the soldiers involved, and Captain Preston, behind bars.

When Captain Preston was absolved from blame, the brothers were not surprised. By then, Patrick Carr's dying confession was public knowledge. Some tried to discredit it, but the truth was the crowd had attacked the soldiers with snowballs and coal, and Captain Preston had stood in front of his men trying to bring calm to a tense situation.

Patrick Carr's testimony was doubly impressive because he was a recent immigrant from Ireland, and probably one of the White Boys, who had rebelled in Ireland and escaped to the colonies to avoid hanging. The White Boys, so-called because of the white hoods they wore to avoid recognition, cut down hedges and fences and re-opened the common grazing pastures to all. The British had almost ruined the Irish, taking over manors, fencing land that had been common grazing or plowed for crops. The British had begun charging rent to the tenants who had farmed for the manor, but who were no longer needed since grazing cattle replaced plowed and harvested fields. So Patrick Carr's last words carried weight. When he said the soldiers had held their fire longer than any time he had seen, he was comparing British soldiers in Ireland, who never hesitated to shoot at rebels, with those he saw in Boston.

Of course, one could only wonder what the whole truth was, since it was only the doctor's retelling of Carr's last words that were heard at Preston's trial.

The second part of the trial would decide the fate of the soldiers. That they were guilty of firing was a given. The question was, did someone give the order? The doctor reported that when Patrick Carr was dying, he said he heard no one give the order, but that the soldiers fired in self-defense. The boys had their doubts. It seemed to them that well-ordered British troops would not have had to fire their weapons.

But these were soldiers who had been battling and losing the battles on the ropewalk. They felt above these common men, and had their pride hurt. They could see in the crowd the very workers who had beaten them with cudgels a few days earlier. And, as testimony showed, other soldiers were equally angry and out of control and perhaps ready to fulfill their warning that many would not be alive in the morning. There were those soldiers who roamed the streets looking for a brawl. There was the skirmish in Boylston's Alley. At Murray's barracks, it took several officers to keep the crowd out and the soldiers in. When all was quiet, a soldier ran out with his gun, damned the people, and threatened to shoot. He was ordered back into the barracks, but then returned minutes later and aimed his rifle at the crowd preparing to fire. Luckily an officer knocked the musket out of his hands. When the bells began to ring, the fire wardens ignored them because they saw there was no fire, only crowds. When others heard the bells, they left their homes to join the fray.

In the soldiers' defense, the crowd probably numbered over five hundred people, some angry about the work issues, others just angry at the presence of British soldiers in Boston. The soldiers formed a semi-circle with muskets lowered, bayonets attached. They were pelted with snowballs and any other items handy, and called names. Most of the crowd was before them, but a few had slipped in behind them. Then the pelting stopped as men with clubs came forward.

These were British soldiers who had come from Ireland, where the rebels meant business and death for the British. So when Hugh Montgomery was knocked aside, his gun fired or he fired his gun. This was followed by more shots. The crowd had yelled, "You do not dare fire!" And perhaps the soldiers heard that and fired, or maybe they just fired at those who had fought them at the ropewalk, or maybe they just fired into the crowd. Some testified that Private Killroy raised his musket and aimed for Sam Gray, his ropewalk enemy. In any event, Sam Gray, Crispus Attucks, and others were killed, while eight were wounded. The jury found only two soldiers guilty of manslaughter, Hugh Montgomery and Matthew Killroy. They could have been hung, but because of the cloudy circumstances, their punishment was mitigated to burning *murderer* on their hand.

Rafe and Gabe did wonder why the soldiers had come with loaded muskets. Was there a secret order to fire on any crowd from the Crown? There had not been the required permission sought from local authorities. The British policy, as understood by the boys, maintained that it took Crown or local permission to fire on citizens, except in cases where they had to fire to protect their lives. Why fire on a crowd throwing snowballs, or even coal? These were not life-threatening objects. Surprisingly not a window was broken in the Custom House, so how was this possible if the soldiers were really under attack by thrown objects? And why did a Captain lead the men? A corporal would have been leader enough. Why were there soldiers in the streets? They should have been in barracks by eight o'clock. If there was real, or perceived-to-be-real, danger, why didn't Captain Preston take a magistrate or officer of the peace with him? The boys found no answers to their questions, but believed firmly that the previous altercations on the ropewalk were a large part of the sad outcome.

The third part of the trial was an attempt to charge Mainwaring and other customs commissioners of firing into the crowd. This was the weakest part of the trial, as there were no solid witnesses to the event, just rumors and propaganda. The commissioners were acquitted as the men had been out of town on the night of the massacre.

Rafe and Gabe thought, 'Well, we had the trial. Was justice served? Did the truth win? Probably. As much as was possible in these insane times. Their unanswered questions would remain just that, unanswered. At least the trial was run fairly. John Adams gave an equitable defense for his clients. The verdict was as fair as it could be. And Boston had shown its character. But, Tucks was still dead, and the British had seemed to have won some kind of victory. Rafe and Gabe thought that now was the time to make the British victory a loss, but a loss without violence—but no action sprang to mind.

Calm before the Storm

When the trial concluded, Father was worried. He expected Gabe to once again fall into a feverish state. He was even more concerned that Rafe and Gabe had somehow turned against him. After Gabe did not collapse, and Rafe did not discuss the trial, Father decided to bring matters into the open. So, during a slow time in the print shop, Father said to Rafe, "Son, I miss our conversations. Even arguments would be better than this silence from thee and Gabe."

Rafe had not enjoyed the silence between them, but he did not want to hurt Father. Now, perhaps it was time to explain. "Father, I have not enjoyed this silence, but I have not known how to speak to thee."

"Just speak, son. Anything would be better than this wall between thee and me."

"As thee knows, Gabe and I have spent much time together." Father nodded. "Gabe and I have had to find a way to understand the life and death of Tucks. How he could be both Crispus Attucks and Michael Johnson."

"I know that is a tough problem," Father agreed. "All I can say is that a man is complex. He is more than his actions at any given time, yet his actions speak for his beliefs."

Rafe continued. "Yes, Father. That was the complexity of Tucks. He was Crispus Attucks, a gentle friend for Gabe, a caring friend for Uncle, and a man aware of the awesome nature of God's creations. Yet, he was also Michael Johnson, who carried a club, who led a group of sailors, who fought soldiers, and died for the poor and their right to work."

Father listened in wonder. His young sons, only fourteen and sixteen, had been forced to reason beyond their youth. He felt angry at Sam Adams and his crowd who had made young boys old beyond their time. What he said was, "That is complex reasoning."

"We've gone further. We have used thy reasoning about violence begetting violence, but have reached a different conclusion."

Father thought, 'Oh no. They have decided violence is an answer.' But he said nothing, wanting to hear his son's thoughts.

"We have decided that it is not the colonist who is at fault. It was not our duty to comply with the British. It was the fault of the British in demanding our compliance. It is their arrogance, their warships, and their troops which have caused these problems and these deaths. It was their demand for taxes that caused the crowds to protest. It was their customs officials' actions that caused men to rebel. We have not spoken of this Father because we did not want to hurt thee. We just disagree with thy conclusions."

Father was quiet for a time. Then, seeing the hurt look on Rafe's face, Father said, "Rafe, I understand that thee believe this. My argument about how the colonists' actions led to violence could just as easily have begun with the actions of the British. I have been afraid to use this argument with thee because I feared thee would choose violence. And, I do not want thee hurt."

"Father," Rafe said, "thee hast taught us well. We take everything we read with a grain of salt. We never did believe what Adams wrote about blood like water running in the streets. We knew the truth lay somewhere between what Captain Preston testified and the patriot's testimony. We know violence leads to violence. But Father, I promised Gabe we would act when the time was right. And there will be a time when we can act without violence. We have to do something for Tucks!"

"I can understand your feelings. I have not liked the way some are portraying Tucks as this violent, unruly man leading gangs of sailors into fights. He was, he is, more than that. But I do not see how thee will find an opportunity to act without violence. I can only urge thee to be careful. I still believe it is better to turn the other cheek when struck," Father said worriedly.

"I do not think we can turn the other cheek anymore. Look at what happened to James Otis. The poor man has some instability in his mind, but the attack in September has driven him to an almost mindless state. What terrible thing did he do except speak his mind for those customs officials and military men to beat him so? He was just sitting in a café on

King Street. Thee can still see the depth of the sword wound a month later. Father, please do not look so hurt. We will never fight or take up arms, but we will find a way to act."

That night at dinner, Gabe asked Father about economics. "Father, I do not understand why there are so many poor people when others seem to do so well. Tucks told me that the unemployment at the docks would cause people not to be able to spend, and that the people whose goods they would usually buy would not be able then to buy goods from others and so on. But when I look around, I do not see merchants or landlords suffering as he said."

"Economics are a little more complex than Tucks saw," Father explained. "Landlords, for example, can have people removed when they cannot pay the rent. But the landlords still own the property and can rent it to someone else, as long as some people have rent money. In many cases the owners live in the place themselves and the rent money is profit. Even if their place remains empty, they can live on their trade. The merchants most affected by the poor are those who sell food and clothing. But, since everyone needs food and clothing, they may still sell their goods to others.

"The other part of economics has to do with money supply. There are only so many gold or silver coins available and the wealthy hold the largest supply." Seeing the questions on Rafe and Gabe's faces, he said, "If you imagine a pan of your mother's cookies: let's say there are a dozen cookies on the pan. The wealthy of our community have ten in their possession. The other two must be divided amongst all the rest of the people. So, those without property, or small businesses, or a trade of some sort, must do without."

Rafe asked angrily, "So, Father, does that mean the poor can be ignored?"

Responding calmly, Father replied, "Of course not. The town is doing what it logically can. Some of the fines and taxes go to give stipends to the 'worthy' poor, or to support apprenticeships in trade or almshouses. And it does cost money to have the guards warn out or send away the poor who come to Boston looking for work and help, but are not citizens of Boston, and who do not have family here. Boston isn't rich enough to help the poor who don't live here."

"What happens to the people who are warned out?" Rafe asked, growing angry with the logical answers to such an emotional issue.

"Some just wander from town to town, sneaking into areas when they can, trying to find relatives when they cannot, or just live in the open and scavenge for what they can find to fill their hungry bellies." Looking at Mother, he said, "Many of the poor are widows, elderly, or women with children. Sometimes if a widow has a home, she will have other poor women live with her. They may spin or weave to earn some money beyond the city stipend. Some poor families are sent to the almshouse where families are split, women to one set of quarters, men to another, and children too young to be apprenticed to another."

"How can they split up families like that?" Rafe questioned.

"Well, some people believe there is no reason to be poor. That the cause is simply a refusal to find work, laziness if you will. The almshouses teach the poor to be hard workers so they can survive on the outside. Men are released to find work. Women have to stay until they have a means of support." Father continued, "In some cases, the poor resort to any means to stay out of the almshouse. They become thieves, or worse."

"Cannot we do something, Father?" Gabe pleaded.

"There are so many in poverty that I cannot imagine what we could do. As early as 1742 our selectmen were trying to support the widows and orphans after the war with Canada. After the French and Indian War there were twelve hundred widows, about one third of the adult females, and women head up twenty percent of all households. There are hundreds of widows from the wars, and hundreds of others who lost their husbands in shipwrecks or from disease. The fire of 1760 alone left over a hundred widows homeless, and most of them were poor to start with. There are women with no sons to take care of them, or no family. And, as thee knows, the harbor ice, cold winters, impressment, and warships have kept many men from finding work. Now that nonimportation is at an end, ships will be built, merchants will be signing on sailors for voyages, and life will be better."

"But, Father, that is the future. What will happen to these poor people in the meantime?"

"They will have to find some way to exist until times are better," Father said reluctantly.

That evening, Mother shared her thoughts with her husband. "Matthew, the children all seem to be obsessed with the poverty around us."

Matthew asked Charity, "All the children?"

"Yes. You heard the boys tonight, and this morning Sarah did the most remarkable thing. You remember the scarf she was knitting?"

"The one she was making to go with her winter coat?'

"The very one. Well, we were sitting at the table in the kitchen. I was catching up on the mending, and Sarah was working on her scarf. She had just decided it was long enough, and had finished the raw edge, when there was a knock at the door. A woman and her child asked if we had any work they could do as the child was hungry. I invited them in and put together soup, bread, a few cookies, milk for the child, and coffee for the woman. As they ate they told their story. Mrs. Clements, Rosemary, and her daughter, Polly, had arrived from Lexington to meet her husband's ship. They went to see his business partner, Mr. Elsener, for the latest details, only to discover the ship, the *Polly*, was believed sunk in a severe storm. 'All our money was tied up in this voyage,' Rosemary said. 'Mr. Elsener said he was bankrupt, and so were we, but not to give up hope on my husband, Bryan, for he is courageous and intelligent, and, if there were any way he could survive the storm, he would.' Rosemary explained, 'Our parents are in Lexington, and Bryan and I were planning to build a home near them after the voyage. I have been looking for work so our daughter and I can stay nearby in case there is any news of my husband. We have used the little money we brought with us and need to find a place to stay and work so we can eat.'

"I sent them to Mrs. Andersen's, she always needs extra help with their eleven children, and would love to have someone live in," Charity added with soft tears coursing down her cheeks.

Matthew knew it was not just for the Clements that Charity cried, but for the children she had lost, and the children she would never have. Her illness had not been as severe as that of Gabe, but had been severe enough to end any hope of more children. Matthew didn't mind about the children. He and Charity had three lovely, intelligent children, and as long as he had Charity, Rafe, Gabe, and Sarah, Matthew was happy. But he did not know how to say this to Charity so she would believe him. He had tried several times, but she felt she had let him down in some way. So this evening he asked, "What about the scarf? What does that have to do with the story?"

"Rosemary and Polly were very grateful for the food and for the directions to the Anderson's. As they were ready to leave, Sarah noticed that Polly had only a worn sweater to keep her warm, so she gave her new scarf to Polly, saying, 'I just finished this and was wondering who I could give it to. Please take this scarf and stay warm.'

"Polly, who hadn't said a word up to this point said shyly, 'Thank you. The scarf is beautiful, and it will keep me warm.' Then the Clements left. I turned to Sarah who said, 'Mother, she needed it and I can make another for me. Besides, is not she one of *the least of these*, like the Bible says?' Yes dear she is, I told her."

"I am so proud of our children!" Matthew said. "I do wish we could do more for the poor. But other than helping those who come to our shop or to our door, I don't know how."

Mother and Sarah

As the days, weeks, and months went by, 1770 was behind them. With the beginning of 1771, the boys resumed their routine of studying and working. Father thought, 'Maybe they have decided I was right.' The supper conversations were back to the pre-massacre level, and even Mother lost her worried look. Gabe seemed healthier, and while he walked the docks for a bit after his studies, he did not return feverish but brightened by the sea air.

One afternoon, Gabe looked unusually concerned when he returned from his walk. Mother realized they had not spoken for some time about Crispus Attucks, and assuming that was the problem, decided to begin a conversation. "Where do thee go these days on thy walks, son?"

Gabe looked up from the floor and said, "Oh, Mother. I walk the wharf and the harbor, and I am so disturbed by what I see. Oh, the sadness!"

Mother was taken aback at this. "What sadness? What disturbs thee so?"

Gabe said, "The poverty I see. May I tell thee what happened when we returned to Tucks's cabin after Uncle had gone?"

Mother nodded yes, and sat down to listen.

"Rafe and I stopped to talk with Mrs. Watson, who always seemed to be hanging out laundry. She did not know where Uncle might have gone, or when, but asked if we were going to live in the cabin now. We were surprised at the question and said 'No, why do you ask?'

"She said, 'I know a young couple, the Nelsons, who have a baby.

They would be willing to rent it from you if the cost is not too dear.' At that, a young sailor and his wife came out of Mrs. Watson's small home. The young wife looked tired and frightened. The young sailor looked angry and nervous. The baby in the young woman's arms looked cold.

"Rafe and I looked at each other and then said, 'We would be pleased to show thee the cabin.' The couple followed us back to Tucks's cabin and when they entered it, the young woman gave out a little gasp. 'It's so neat!' she exclaimed. Then, turning to her husband, Jean said, 'Luke, do you think we can afford something as grand as this?' He looked at her and replied, 'I am not sure.' Turning to Rafe and I he asked, 'Is there some extra work we can do for you to lower the price? We do not have a lot of money.' I spoke up and said, 'Don't worry about money. The cabin is thine.' Rafe nodded in agreement.

"Rafe then lit a fire. I walked the woman over to the chair, put the afghan around her shoulders, then had her husband bring the bench near to the fire and we all sat down. I told the young couple about Crispus Attucks. I did not say he had been a slave only that he had been a sailor. As Jean fingered the afghan I told her that Tucks's mother had made the afghan and the quilts. I showed the sea chest to Luke, and Jean noticed the Bible on the shelf and the handmade dishes. She said, 'A sailor lived here alone?'

"Yes, I answered. The only rent Rafe and I demanded was that if an old sailor came to the door, they were to take him in and care for him as long as he stayed. Jean looked a bit frightened, so I told the story of Uncle. I also said she probably would never see him, but that Crispus Attucks would want Uncle to be cared for. Luke could not believe that was all we wanted for rent. Rafe said that if he had rent money, he should try to help others as we were helping them. There was lots of wood around and other cabins could be built for more families. Luke looked pleased. He said, 'When I am not at sea, I will build.' They thanked us. We said, 'Remember Crispus Attucks as a good man. If thee hear ill of him, think of the good he has done for Uncle and for thee.' Then Rafe said, 'Gabe walks the harbor for his health. He will check on thee once in a while and if thee need anything send word to the Bellson print shop.'

"Since then, Mother, I have seen more and more families without food, or shelter, or proper clothing. There is so little I can do. It hurts my heart. Uncle said Crispus Attucks died for those people. I do not understand why their lives are so hard."

Mother said, "I do not either, Gabe." As he left to take his afternoon nap, she pondered what he had said. She looked up to see Sarah standing there. "Sarah, did you hear our conversation?"

"I did, Mother. There must be something we can do."

"I think so too, Sarah. I think so too."

Mother and Sarah had heard the urgency in Gabe's voice, and seen the anger in Rafe's questions to Father about the poor, and the few and unacceptable options available to them to gain any help, and their faces as Father further explained the economics of poverty and its hopelessness. The women were sure the boys were thinking of Luke and Jean in Crispus Attucks's little cabin.

Later over cleaning and dishes, Charity and Sarah decided to find Mrs. Watson and Jean. Maybe there was something women could do that the men had not considered.

Rafe also decided to act, only he would go to the Sons of Liberty and attend their weekly meetings beginning the next evening.

Gabe wondered, 'Why is there poverty? Even Jesus himself had said, *The poor you will have with you always.* God cannot want people to be in poverty, so why will there always be poor people?'

It was thirteen-year-old Sarah who said it first, "Mother, we women *have* acted throughout this time of turmoil. We have refused to purchase British goods and shop where British goods were being sold. Other women too have refused to purchase British goods and to sell them. We are stronger than Father thinks. I cannot bear to see Gabe carry this burden alone and I fear Rafe may do something rash. They helped a couple by giving them Tucks's cabin. We gave food to Uncle when he was ill. Surely we can do something more substantial!"

Mother listened thoughtfully, then spoke. "Well, child—or should I say young lady? Thee has said much of what I was thinking. I may not have signed a boycott agreement but I have not served tea to our family; in fact, I gave Uncle the last of the tea we had in the cupboard."

"Yes," Sarah replied. "And you taught me to spin and weave and all our new clothes are homespun. Not only that, but our knit scarves and gloves are warmer than any British goods. Say Mother, maybe that is a way. We could get women together to make clothing, or at least scarves and gloves, for the poor."

"That is a great start. I know several women who would like to help. But I still want to find Mrs. Watson and Jean. Do thee think thee can lead me to them?"

"Thee knew I followed the boys, did thee not?"

"Of course. Thy errands always took longer when the boys had gone to see Uncle."

"Well, it will serve us in good stead. I know where Mrs. Watson is for sure; she always has laundry on the line."

Mother replied, "It is my thought that she does laundry to support or help support her family. She took in Luke, Jean, and the baby. She must have ideas for us."

Sarah led Mother toward the wharf. She got confused at first, about the direction to the harbor cabins, but then saw the white blowing in the breeze and was sure it was Mrs. Watson's laundry on the line. When they arrived, they found an exhausted woman, frustrated at the situation she and others found themselves in. How could the town let this happen? Why did they not act to help those made poor by the soldiers taking the only work available?

Mary Watson invited Charity and Sarah into the summer kitchen and to the warmth the stove and canvas provided. She invited them to sit on one of the benches while she finished hanging out the last few items. She bragged that her husband had invented the idea of using canvas around the summer kitchen and of using rope to hang clothing from.

Charity and Sarah had time to look around and were surprised by the small industry before them. Twelve-year-old Hope was adding laundry to the boiling water on the stove at the center of the room. Nine-year-old Faith and seven-year-old Lovey were folding clothes on a table near one end of the room. They saw the clean and folded laundry in labeled baskets and placed on one of a series of shelves built into the wall. Hope looked up from the pot of boiling water and smiled at Mrs. Bellson and Sarah, then shyly moved to help her sisters fold laundry.

In a few minutes Mary returned and said to the Bellsons, "I will be right with you." Then she turned to the girls, "You are doing a fine job. We are almost done, just this last load to scrub and hang. Hope, can you take care of that for me?" Hope smiled and nodded her head yes. "When you each are done with your work, come inside and join us."

Mary Watson removed her fingerless gloves and handed them to Hope who had removed the clothes from the boiling water, scrubbed and rinsed them, and was ready to hang the clothes outside. Mary then dipped each hand in grease, rubbed the grease in a bit, and then put on a pair of full-fingered gloves. Seeing the questioning looks, Mary explained, "If I do not use the grease, my hands become raw, then split and bleed on the laundry. The gloves protect my hands and my livelihood. Let us go inside and have coffee."

After accepting a cup of coffee, Charity explained her need to help the poor and Sarah her idea of making scarves or other warm things.

Mrs. Watson told the women she felt overwhelmed by the depth of the problem, the sheer numbers of the poor. Except for taking in a couple now and then, or providing a meal for someone, she did not know what else she could do. With the nonimportation acts by the colonists, the price of clothing was out of reach. The poorest had no spinning wheels or looms and were in desperate need of warm clothing. They needed food and shelter too, but for the most part those not in the almshouses would rather starve than go there and face the breakup of their family.

Mrs. Watson pointed to what had been Tucks's cabin. There was only a little smoke coming from the chimney.

Sarah asked, "Why do not Luke and Jean have a larger fire today? It is cold."

Mrs. Watson replied, wiping tears from her eyes. "The Nelson's baby died two days after they settled in, probably from the two nights spent in the open. Since the burial Jean just sits and stares at the floor. She does not clean, or cook, or wash. She just sits. Luke stays with her as much as he can, for she lets the fire go out, but he needs to find work and so must leave her alone at times."

"Their story is fairly typical. When Luke earned money as an able seaman, they rented nice rooms for a time, and were able to save a bit. After the British arrived and ice covered the harbor, and no ships were sailing, he found work on the ropewalk, until all the trouble. Since he earned less on land than he did at sea, they moved to attic rooms for less rent. By watching their money carefully they were able to stay in the attic—until the landlord asked them to leave so his son and wife could move in as his son had no work.

"Luke, Jean, and the baby were given three days to find another place. They could not find one they could afford, and so spent two nights huddled under a fishing boat along the harbor. I saw them shivering in the cold and brought them home with me. The Nelsons had only been here one day when your boys stopped by. I thought the boys were a godsend. But their kindness was too late for the baby, and maybe for the mother. So many good people have been hurt by the arrival of the British and it has been such a hard winter." Mrs. Watson finished by saying. "I do what I can but the problem is beyond me. I do not know what you folks can do to help, but food and warm clothing would be a blessing."

Charity explained that they planned to have women join them to spin and knit scarves, socks, and gloves. They hoped they could bring the goods to Mrs. Watson and she could distribute the items to the poor.

Mrs. Watson smiled and said, "I might not have the time for distribution, but I have an idea about who might have the time. Let me work on my idea. You can bring the finished items here."

Sarah's idea seemed to be the way to help. Mother gathered her Quaker friends. They talked, they laughed, and they made thread and yarn. Anyone with a spinning wheel was welcome, and if a person did not know how to spin, they were taught. Sarah and her friends were never without some sort of needlework. Even conversations after dinner were accompanied by the clicking of needles, as scarf after scarf was completed.

The *Boston Gazette* interpreted their acts and those of other women as ones of patriotism, saying, "The industry and frugality of American ladies must exalt their character in the Eyes of the World and serve to show how greatly they are contributing to bring about the political salvation of a whole continent."

Some of the wealthier women, wanting to support the nonimportation of British goods, began employing poor women to sew their clothing. Some merchants loaned spinning wheels and purchased the spun thread which they then put out to weavers. More than 170,000 yards of homespun were purchased before the repeal of the Townsend Act. For some, independence from British goods continued to be their aim, and many a poor woman now supplied with equipment and a purchaser could spin and remain at home to support her family.

Sarah and Mother felt they were making a difference. They knew that their actions and those of other women like them helped the poorest of the poor. If even a few mothers could stay home to work and care for their children that was better than it had been before, when the youngest of children as well as both parents strove to find paying work to put food on the table.

That many still wandered, or remained in poverty, came from foolish laws and a mistaken idea about poverty. Mother and daughter often thought out loud together, "What good was done by putting a man into jail because he could not pay his debts? Would he earn the money there? And what of his family, would they not just be placed on the relief rolls? And almshouses, why separate families? Would not a man work harder to keep his family fed and clothed? What was the almshouse's incentive? And the warnings out? If a family was poor, a woman could not leave to go to her family for help, she had to stay with her husband. The man could not go to his wife's family for help, because he did not have residence where his wife's family lived. How did these poverty laws help anyone?"

So, if the law couldn't or wouldn't help, an individual might. After three weeks, Sarah, Rafe, and Charity returned to the home of Mrs. Watson. Mary told them her idea and it was agreed that Rafe would approach Jean with their needs. When Rafe arrived at the cabin, Jean was cleaning up after lunch. Her eyes were red from crying, and though she was out of her chair and moving about, her countenance plainly showed the depth of her depression. Jean welcomed Rafe, however, saying Uncle had not ever arrived.

Rafe took the chair she offered, and began by saying, "Jean, I know thee and Luke have been through great sadness, but I have a problem I hope you can help me with."

Jean said, "You have been so generous, Luke. I would do anything to help you if we can."

"I know Luke needs to find work," Rafe began. "It is thy help I need right now. My sister and mother and their friends have been knitting and sewing and have completed a large quantity of items to be handed to the poorest of those in need. We don't have the time to hand them out, and we know with certainty that Mary with her laundry business does not have time to deliver the items either. We are hoping we can depend on thee."

Jean was thoughtful, and did not say anything for a while. Rafe waited patiently, hoping his offer would be accepted and that this might raise Jean out of her depression. Finally Jean looked up, she said, "I don't know if I can."

Rafe responded, "Then why not come with me to Mrs. Watson's and together maybe we can find a solution?" Jean agreed, though she felt nervous about leaving the cabin. She had not seen anyone or been anywhere since their baby died.

Mary Watson was pleased to see Jean. Jean shyly thanked Mrs. Watson for her kindness after the baby's death. Both women expressed their pleasure at the number and quality of items the Bellsons had brought. At Mrs. Watson's nod, Rafe, Charity, and Sarah rose to take their leave. Mrs. Watson said, "Thank you. Jean and I can figure this out. Keep up the excellent work. Your items will save many from the cold."

As Sarah and Charity left, they immediately began making plans for more items. Rafe looked back to see young Hope waving good-bye to him from the doorway. She called, "Come back soon."

And they did come back soon. Every three weeks Charity, Sarah, or Rafe would take the finished items to the home of Mrs. Watson. Mary told them that she and Jean had delivered the first group of items together. The next time Jean did it alone. Later, Jean had set up a sewing circle in her home with the women and children they had helped. Jean grew happier and healthier, and finally rounder, as she became pregnant with another child.

Rafe, especially, enjoyed taking the finished items to the Watson home whenever Father could spare him from the printing business. Seventeen-year-old Rafe found in twelve-year-old Hope the fun and laughter he missed, especially now that Gabe was studying for Harvard. He mused that hard work made some people serious and others full of energy and joy. He found that joy in Hope and looked forward to his time with her.

He also filled in for Luke and John when they were at sea, now that the harbor was cleared, for there were always repairs to be made and wood to cut for the two families. John and Mary's mothers found his visits calming. Rafe was always willing to sit with them, sometimes sorting material for their weaving, sometimes reading from the Bible, and sometimes just sharing the news of 1771 and 1772.

Sam Adams

At sixteen, when Gabe took a break from his studies, he often walked the wharf and sometimes listened on the fringes of the groups surrounding Mr. Samuel Adams. Adams seemed to really know and understand the problems of the people. He was giving them hope as things were starting to turn around, but he also warned that the tax on tea was the same as any tax. If Parliament were to get away with this tax, they would be able to use the tea tax as a foundation to add more taxes. It was a speech Gabe had heard often. This day, Gabe listened and then remained after Adams's talk with the dock workers and sailors.

"Now what liberty can there be where property is taken away without consent? Can it be said with any color of truth and justice, that this continent of three thousand miles in length, and of a breadth as yet unexplored, in which, however, it is supposed there are five millions of people, has the least voice, vote, or influence in the British Parliament? Have they all together any more weight or power to return a single member to that House of Commons who have not inadvertently, but deliberately, assumed a power to dispose of their lives, liberties, and properties, than to choose an Emperor of China? Had the Colonists a right to return members to the British Parliament, it would only be hurtful; as from their local situation and circumstances, it is impossible they should ever be truly and properly represented there. The inhabitants of this country, in all probability, in a few years will be more numerous than those of Great Britain and Ireland together; yet it is absurdly expected by the promoters of the present measures that these, with their posterity to all generations, should be easy, while their property shall be disposed of by a House of Commons at three

thousand miles' distance from them, and who cannot be supposed to have the least care or concern for their real interest; who have not only no natural care for their interest, but must be in effect bribed against it, as every burden they lay on the Colonists is so much saved to gain to themselves. Hitherto, many of the colonists have been free from quit rents, but if the breath of a British House of Commons can originate an act for taking away all our money, our lands will go next, or be subject to rack rents from haughty and relentless landlords, who will ride at ease, while we are trodden in the dirt. The Colonists have been branded with the odious names of traitors and rebels only for complaining of their grievances. How long such treatment will or ought to be borne is submitted."

As he concluded his speech, Adams noticed the boy, and connected him with Crispus Attuck. He wondered why this lad was still walking the wharves since the lad's father had said he was well.

After answering all the questions his listeners had to ask, Adams turned to Gabe and asked, "Well, boy, it's Gabe, is not it?"

Gabe replied, "Yes, sir."

"What are you doing around here? My talks cannot be that exciting. I have been told all I say is the same thing over and over: 'Beware of Parliament'!"

"It is not the speech, Mr. Adams," Gabe responded. "I was looking for a chance to speak with thee ... about Crispus Attucks, and about other things."

"Come on, lad. Take me to that ship of yours—what do you call it? Ah, the *Intrepid*."

Gabe was pleased. He and Mr. Adams strolled in the sun, and found a quiet place to sit on Gregson's Wharf near the *Intrepid*. Adams asked about the ship and Gabe explained why his father had built it, and the lessons he and Rafe had learned from the ship. As the boy talked, Sam Adams remembered his own youth climbing to his father's observatory to watch ships, and then later wandering the harbor, pestering sailors until they let him aboard their ships.

When Gabe finished explaining, he said, "Mr. Adams, thee art sitting where Crispus Attucks, my Tucks, used to sit."

Adams looked around, and said, "He was a fine man. He cared about the problems of the poor. He also was angry, angry at the impressment, the arrogance of the British, the lack of work, the soldiers taking the little work available, and more. I always felt that your Tucks really understood what our struggle with the British is all about. You know many people believe I encouraged or even organized the crowds that night. I did not. They did not need me to be angry enough to act." He paused, then said, "Did you know I often read your journal?"

When Gabe looked puzzled, Mr. Adams said, "Your father shared it with me. Sometimes I smiled when you wrote that there was an article that sounded like Crispus Attucks in print. You see, some of my best ideas came from the things Tucks shared with you."

"Thee wrote what Tucks told me?" Gabe wondered at this. A part of him was upset that his father had shared his journal. On the other hand, to think that the thoughts of Crispus Attucks were in the paper for all to see!

Mr. Adams continued, "That's why I called his death a Bloody Massacre. I knew that the soldiers were protecting themselves, but if they had been properly under control they would never have fired into a crowd, and they never should have left the barracks with loaded muskets. I also knew that Crispus Attucks had changed. He barely controlled his anger after the Snyder boy was killed. I think he always thought it could have been you. He loved you very much."

Gabe, choked back tears as he spoke. "I loved him too. My family feels I should get over the pain of my loss of a good friend, but I cannot. How can I?"

Samuel Adams thought long and hard before answering. "Gabe, some losses you never get over. I have lost a wife and children and while I know my God is always with me and has blessed me with another wife, I still feel the pain. But, I have learned there are truths that need to be told, and causes that need to be fought, and so I write and I fight for my beliefs.

"I know from your father that you are scheduled for Harvard. Go. Give it your all. There is much to do in this world, good causes to fight for, and there is always truth to be told. The pain will lessen as you find meaningful work to do."

Gabe listened to this man who seemed to feel the same pain that he felt. Then, after a pause, he gathered his courage and said, "Mr. Adams, as I walk the wharf I see men out of work and families without homes— can thee explain this to me?"

Adams thought before answering, and said, "The easy answer is there is not enough work that pays a decent wage so a man can support his family. The harder answer is one of economics."

Gabe interrupted, "Do not thee tell me that. That is all my father can talk about."

"Well, Gabe. I do not know what your father has told you, but let me share what I believe. For the typical poor person there is an aspect of society that has let them down."

"What do thee mean, 'let them down.'"

"Let me see if I can explain. Let us suppose you are a sailor and sign articles to work on a ship. You have signed yourself into the care and protection of the ship's captain. He agrees to bring you back home. He will pay you a wage you both agree upon, and you agree to serve aboard the ship and follow orders. At home, your wife and children wait for the captain to bring their loved one back home. But the ship comes home without him. What happened? Disease is the usual answer, so did the captain err and enter a port where disease was rampant? Or, it could have been a storm. Did the captain sail the ship in a way that the storm did as little damage as possible, or not? So many things could have caused the loved one's death but, the sailor is not brought home as promised.

"Now, what happens to the widow and her children? Is there no responsibility on the part of the captain to see that they are taken care of, especially since he promised to bring the sailor home and his errors could have led to the sailor's death? If it is not the captain's fault, then what about the ship's owner, or the merchant who began the voyage to sell his goods? Shouldn't someone be responsible for the family since the sailor did not come home?"

Gabe said, "Someone should help them, but does not a sailor know that any voyage is dangerous? Should not he have made sure his wife and children would be cared for if something happened?"

"Good question. Now, how could he do that? Does he make enough money to be sure that they will be cared for if he does not return? No." Mr. Adams continued, "I am not saying that any one of the people in our example is at fault. Society is at fault. Why should a person become dependent on the city's stipend or be placed in an almshouse because they are poor through no fault of their own?" He paused. "I have no answer to my questions, or to yours. I have only questions and more questions. But the example I gave is that of the 'worthy' poor."

Gabe looking puzzled, "Can someone be an 'unworthy' poor?"

"Yes, a person can drink or refuse jobs that are available. This person is the kind for which the almshouses were created. I am only sorry to see so many good people forced to enter them."

"So, what is the answer? Thee cannot have only questions."

"You are right, Gabe I do have an idea, an idea for this time to defy Parliament, to gain independence from Great Britain, but most of all an idea of the future. I want to see a world where all men are equal.

Where every child is educated. Where workers and owners solve problems together. Where justice is fair to all. You know I am a religious man; well, it is sin that keeps us apart. Old-fashioned greed and envy and pride keep us from working together to a common end. When we realize that and really do work together, there is nothing we cannot achieve in America."

"That's what Tucks said," Gabe said eagerly.

"And he was right. That's why I go around talking to anyone who will listen. My message is the same: Parliament is the enemy. If we all boycott British products, Parliament will have to back down. But people do not want to give up their tea. Is not that strange? Independence may rest upon a cup of tea." Looking at Gabe he said, "I do not think I have answered your question about why there are poor people."

"I guess there is not a simple answer. Would thee be willing to talk to my brother, Rafe, sometime?"

Mr. Adams said, "Anytime I am free. You know, Gabe, you and your brother are very special people. I think you should be called 'special' not 'peculiar.'"

As he and Gabe parted, Samuel Adams thought of the children he had lost, and wondered if a Samuel or a Joseph or a Mary would have been like Gabriel or Rafael. And if his wife Elizabeth had not died ... but that was in the past. He had a wonderful family now, and work to do!

Gabe thought about his future, and how difficult for a person to ever get over losing a wife or child. He could not imagine life without Mother, or Sarah, or Rafe. How empty he and Father would feel. Just like he felt now, missing Tucks. Could he find work to do as Mr. Adams suggested? Worthwhile work to do, or truth to tell?

As he watched Gabe walk away, Adams thought about the last few years. He regretted the violence of the past. He saw that it had gained the colonies nothing. Part of the violence could have been prevented, but some of the violence escalated from the eagerness to bring change.

The Sons of Liberty

For Rafe, the problem of poverty was one of lack of action. He had been reading about the Sons of Liberty. Their name came from a speech in Parliament given by Colonel Issac Barre, when he said, 'Those sons of liberty across the Atlantic will fight the new tax law.' The Sons of Liberty were not made up from ignorant mobs. Instead their membership in all colonies included intellectuals; small, inter-colonial merchants; and artisans. The intellectuals seemed to look to the future. Rafe had heard that Sam Adams's dream was to create a "Christian Sparta, a place where hardy, self-denying, God-fearing people would think of the public, not of themselves." For the merchants and artisans a strong economy was the goal, and they supported nonimportation of British goods so that their own goods might sell. The overall goal seemed to be to help the individual worker to understand that British laws affected them. The Sons of Liberty wanted the average man to begin to question in his heart what America should be.

In Boston, the Sons of Liberty focused on fighting the British with words, crowds, and with boycotts. This happened in other colonies too, but elsewhere the Sons of Liberty also fought against poor wages and unemployment. In the *New York Journal*, the essays were about the evils of high rents, rising prices, and short employment; they wrote of popular uprisings in London to resist the price of grain; and opposed the imprisonment of debtors. The essays made fun of fashionable young men who would not wear homespun. A New Yorker wrote, "Some individuals … by the Smiles of Providence, or some other means, are enabled to roll in their four whell'd Carriages, and can support the expense of good Houses, rich Furniture, and Luxurious Living. But is it equitable that 99, rather 999, should suffer for the Extravagance or Grandeur of one? Especially when it is considered that Men frequently owe their Wealth to the impoverishment of their Neighbors?"

In Connecticut the issues included paper money and speculators. In each colony, the Sons of Liberty developed in different ways, with different issues, but they remained in contact with each other, and pledged cooperation with each other.

After Gabe's conversation with Mr. Adams, Rafe had done some research and was pleased with what he discovered. He liked that Adams was a religious man, even if that meant he was Puritan, for it was the Puritans who had ousted the Quakers so many years ago. Sam's father was a deacon in their church and active in politics, so that's probably where Sam acquired his understanding of how to make politics work for his cause. Adams was no businessman—unsuccessful at each attempt— and spent much time poor. Even now his home and clothing said "limited means."

But probably his anger toward the British came from his father's experience, and later his own experience fighting to hold onto whatever of his father's property he could. His father and friends had formed a land bank, literally a bank whose worth was based on the amount of land they owned. The British, with the aid of men like Thomas Hutchinson (now Governor Hutchinson), shut down the bank, and Adams's father and his father's friends were left with huge debts to pay. The Hutchinsons had always used their money and influence to run things their way and now they were actively supporting the British with taxation of the colonies.

Sam Adams was against this new policy of customs' duties, for while they had been raised at first to support trade, they were now used as a means of raising money for England. As early as 1768, Adams had written to then governor Bernard that the purpose of government was "To promote to the utmost of their power the welfare of the subject, and support his Majesty's authority within this jurisdiction; to make a thorough inquiry into the Grievances of the people to have them redressed; To amend, strengthen and preserve the laws of the land; To reform illegal proceedings in administration and support the public liberty." He had explained the protests as the voice of the people; "the very supposition of an unwillingness in the people in general, that a law should be executed, carries with it the strongest presumption, that it is an unjust law."

If Bernard or Hutchinson had listened to the people, if they had made a "thorough inquiry into the Grievances of the people," then the colony would not be in the shape it was. Rafe respected Mr. Adams more and more as he read his words.

Rafe spent his time looking up the *Massachusetts Charter of 1691*—a contract between the King and the colony that gave the colony the right to tax itself. Nowhere did it state that Parliament had the right to levy taxes on the colony of Massachusetts. Rafe also began to understand the reason for the half-truths in the recent essays. The government, both in England and in America, had not listened to the people's rational arguments. The choice left was to call the people to action by whatever means were necessary, and for Mr. Adams those means were words.

Mr. Adams was a well-educated man. He had attended Boston Latin School, as Gabe had, and then Harvard, as Gabe would in the fall. Mr. Adams had earned a master's degree from Harvard, something almost unheard of. His business losses were almost unheard of too. Whoever heard of a businessman or tax collector who would not press clients for the amount due? When Sam spoke to Gabe about society's role in poverty, he was probably thinking about a time when he was so poor his children and he depended on neighbors to eat. This Mr. Adams really did understand poverty. And he had fought to make money more available to people. It was clear from what he had told Gabe that he truly wanted a "virtuous, egalitarian society." But whether that would ever happen, Rafe did not know. He wanted to speak with this man. He needed to speak with this man. Despite this desire, they seldom had time to talk when Mr. Adams came into the shop, and Mr. Adams seemed busy most every evening.

Rafe had read Adams's essay on the "Mysteries of Government." Though it was written in 1769, it seemed to be speaking to the present. Rafe enjoyed reading the historical development of rights and their relation to the chain of government. His favorite part was:

> ... at the revolution, the British constitution was again restored to its original principles, declared in the bill of rights; which was afterwards passed into a law, and stands as a bulwark to the natural rights of subjects. 'To vindicate these rights,' says Mr. Blackstone, 'when actually violated or attacked, the subjects of England are entitled—first, through the regular administration and free course of justice in the courts of law—next, to the right of petition to the King and parliament for redress of grievances—and lastly, to the right of having and using arms for self-preservation and

defense.' These he calls 'auxiliary subordinate rights, which serve principally as barriers to protect and maintain inviolate the three great and primary rights of personal security, personal liberty, and private property': And that of having arms for their defense he tells us is 'a public allowance, under due restrictions, of the natural right of resistance and self-preservation, when the sanctions of society and laws are found insufficient to restrain the violence of oppression.'

Rafe especially liked the restriction on violence and its use as a last resort. Rafe did not want to see violence rule, and if the time came, he would have no part of violence, though he would do all he could to help remove the British.

As time slipped away, so did the chance for action. Despite Mr. Adams's best efforts, the nonimportation agreements by colonies were relaxed. By October of 1770, any protests against the Townsend Acts were at an end. Trade with Britain was restored and there was prosperity in the harbors. Even the loyalists and patriots were able to work together to move the city's powder house to a safer location.

It seemed the colonies were fighting amongst themselves instead of against the British.

Rafe and Gabe

At sixteen, Gabe left home for Harvard. He heard from Rafe each week, by letter, about the progress being made to help the poor. Rafe believed that the new prosperity in the harbors would provide labor for all those ready and able to work.

Gabe was able to find a second home-away-from-home with Aunt Ruth, his mother's sister. As he searched his mind for the important work he was to do, Gabe realized he needed to understand himself first. So he asked Aunt Ruth about her other sister, his Aunt Martha, realizing she was a significant part of his history. Gabe felt badly that he couldn't remember the woman who had cared for him when he was so ill, and had wondered if his illness caused Martha's death in childbirth, though he hadn't said this out loud to anyone before.

Aunt Ruth, seeing the need in his face, reassured him. "No, Gabe. The time she spent in your home was one of her favorite memories. You see, Martha always felt your mother was the weak one of the family. Charity had been ill several times as a child, and once we thought she would die. When she grew into a lovely woman and married your father we were all so pleased! Then came the pregnancies. You are old enough to know that Sarah wasn't the last child, only the last child who lived. Eventually there weren't more pregnancies. But each miscarriage made your mother weaker. When you were so ill, Martha felt she might lose both a sister and a nephew, so she insisted on moving in to help. But Charity was stronger than Martha knew, as were you."

"But, Aunt Martha died while I was still ill—are thee sure I was not responsible?" Gabe asked.

"Yes, I am sure. You were ill a very long time, and your Aunt Martha was barely pregnant when she stayed with your family. Gabe, Martha loved children and had as many as she could. But sometimes, after a woman has a certain number of children, her body just gives out and she dies while giving birth."

"I feel better now, but what makes it so hard for me is I have almost no memory of her, and little memory of the time I was ill."

"Gabe, you wouldn't have memories of Martha. Because they had five children, Martha and Albert travelled very little. She did come to help your mother after each of you were born, but you were only two when Sarah was born. Even though you were ten when you became ill, you were much too ill to remember Martha's care of you.

"You are not responsible for her death. Even if it had been the illness that made a difference, you would not have been responsible! Now, why don't you get settled in for the night? I'll bring some warm milk to help you sleep."

'Dear Aunt Ruth,' Gabe thought. 'How lucky I am to be able to stay with thee!'

Aunt Ruth was pleased to have Gabe stay with her. She had never married. Hers was a familiar story: she fell in love, and he was killed in the French and Indian War. Unlike other young women, Ruth had never fallen in love again, and no one had sought her out. Her aunt and uncle had no children; so they left their home to Ruth. She had opened her home to boarders, which gave her the opportunity to do what she loved best: cook and become a part of others' lives. Lately she had become lonesome. Gabe gave Ruth a reason to write weekly reports to Charity and Matthew.

Gabe was equally pleased. He had many issues to talk through. Aunt Ruth was family, so she would listen. She didn't have all the details of his history with Crispus Attucks and Uncle, so she would be unbiased as she listened. And Gabe felt the need for an unbiased listener: one who wouldn't be afraid that excitement would make him unwell; one who could sense his feelings, hear the honesty of them, and accept them without fear of some illness to follow. He needed his Aunt Ruth; he needed to share with someone. 'Is not this strange? My mother, my sister, my brother, my father all love me, all know me—and yet, I feel the need for someone to listen.'

Even more than the demands of Harvard, Gabe felt the need to move beyond the constraints of Boston and the Granary Burial Ground where Crispus Attucks lay buried with Christopher Snyder and the other massacre victims. Crispus would love that he was buried with young Snyder. It was the young boy's death that had been a catalyst for Tucks's own death.

As the warm milk began to fill his body with the comfort that leads to rest, Gabe wondered what young Polly Clements was doing. The last time he saw her, months ago now, he had been wandering through the market on his way to visit Tucks. They had only waved and smiled, but Gabe had felt warmed by this unusual friendship.

He wouldn't have known Polly Clements if it hadn't been for his sister. Sarah had given her scarf to Polly, and by an accidental meeting at the market in Faneuil Hall, had become best friends, meeting each week on shopping day. One Thursday, when Polly was to do her shopping, Sarah rested in his window seat recovering from a nasty cold. She begged Gabe to meet Polly and explain why she couldn't be there. He was also to spend some time with Polly and find out the latest news on her father and his ship before he headed to the wharf. Gabe did so. Sarah had done so many things for Gabe it was the least he could do to spend an hour or so with Polly. The "hour or so" turned into most of the morning. Polly was easy to talk with and eager to share her memory of that first meeting with the Bellsons.

Polly said, "My mother and I left Mr. Elsener's business office in shock. To think my father and his ship might be lost! Mother was determined to remain in Boston until there was a final answer to the question of what had happened to father. We headed immediately to your print shop and home, as Mr. Elsener said if anyone would know where to find work and lodging it was Charity Bellson. Your path was so inviting, and the flowers so cheering, we hardly minded the cold. Sarah said you and Rafe created the walkway."

"Yes," Gabe replied. "Rafe wanted a walk that kept visitors out of the mud, so we hauled rock and sand from the shore, dug holes to level the rocks, and filled it all in with sand and crushed shells. But it was Sarah who planted the flowers near the gate. She said our wattle fence was sturdy but ugly, and needed flowers to invite people into the garden and kitchen."

"She was so right! The path, the flowers, the gate with its welcome sign, and the wonderful garden—all neat rows with flowers amidst the vegetables. I loved the colorful chicken shed in the back of the garden."

Gabe laughed. "That was made from old shipping crates. It was

Sarah's idea to paint each one with different colors. She even went around and bargained for leftover paint, only taking the colors she liked. I wondered about green, yellow, and blue, but in the end the colors worked together. It was the apricot that set the colors in unison."

Polly laughed. "It was all so wonderful, and so different from what I expected. Your mother and Sarah were different from what I expected too. I think I expected a colorless, serious woman, since Mr. Elsener said you were Quakers. But your home was welcoming, and your mother soft, though not as colorful as the chicken shed." Here Gabe and Polly both laughed. "Still more wonderful than I could have hoped. Mother and I weren't used to being on the receiving end of charity, but your mother helped out of friendship and love, not out of our need. Does that make sense, Gabe?"

"It does. I've seen people give 'charity' that sometimes makes me cry, and I'm only an onlooker. There is no need to make the person receiving help feel guilty, or embarrassed for having to ask for help. That kind of giving isn't charity. True charity is seeing the need and filling it before someone has to ask for help, or at least solving the problem and not asking the other person to humble herself."

"I know exactly what you mean, Gabe." Polly interjected. "Your mother invited us in; she and Sarah took our wraps, set us down by the fire, and gave us coffee. We spoke of many things, as though we were old friends, before my mother got to the reason for our visit. Your mother's advice was perfect, and we gained housing and employment at the Anderson's home."

Gabe felt he could still hear her laughter, and her sadness. All she had heard about her father was that his ship had landed in Port-o-Prince, unloaded its cargo, and loaded another cargo for the return voyage, and that was three days before a bad storm hit the islands. As Gabe drifted off to sleep, he said a prayer for Polly and her mother. For Bryan Clements and all the men at sea, he prayed for soft winds and an early return to port.

Rafe was lonelier than he had imagined he would be without Gabe. Sometimes in the evening, he would visit Charles Cotter, the apprentice who had stayed on to teach him how to become a printer. Charles and

Rafe had become close friends during Rafe's training. Charles was also a member of the Sons of Liberty. Rafe, missing Gabe, joined Charles at meetings and brought a calming, logical influence on the other young men.

When he was fully accepted into the group, Rafe was able to bring up for discussion the unruly crowds and the vandalism and violence they had committed in the past. Most of the young men were looking for some kind of mischief against those who continued to import British goods; Rafe was able to softly and gently question what damage their mischief might do, and to remind them what the mischief of the past had done to Boston's reputation. The young men gradually listened to their new friend, and began to consider other ways to make their point with importers. None of them wanted a repeat of what had happened to the Snyder boy, yet it seemed something needed to be done.

Rafe attended meetings, counseled reason, and longed to speak with Samuel Adams. He felt lonely, and spent long hours reading everything he could. Being informed, being aware of what people were thinking, listening to their talk, watching their body language, that was the way to help the efforts of those like himself who wanted so desperately to act. Rafe sent letter after letter to Gabe at Harvard, and received letter after letter in return. By the time action was possible, the groundwork, the network, and the communication had already been established.

Rafe found himself visiting the Watson's home more and more often. He loved the laughter of their oldest daughter. Hope was a good name for her, she gave him hope for the future, her blond curls bouncing as she folded laundry. He often accompanied her as she picked up and delivered laundry, and in some locations it was good that he did. Fourteen-year-old Hope was getting to the age where men began to look at her as a woman, not as a child, and that could be dangerous. At some point Mary, Hope's mother, asked if he would mind walking Hope to certain destinations on a weekly basis. Since they were after-business hours at the print shop, Rafe was eager to comply. He needed this positive young woman in his life. He needed someone to look out for now that Gabe was at Harvard. Unfortunately, when John Watson was home, he took over the deliveries and Rafe had fewer reasons to visit.

Perhaps that was just as well. In 1773, Rafe was finally able to meet with Sam Adams, and while all of his questions weren't answered, a plan of action began to grown in Rafe's mind.

Reflections: Deeper and Deeper

Connecticut and Pennsylvania were arguing over territory, as were New Hampshire and New York. Most colonies had boundaries that extended unending to the West. But the West was now considered Indian land, as the British had closed the frontier beyond the Appalachian Mountains after the French and Indian War. Men who had fortunes waiting for them in that West, saw those fortunes ebbing away as the 1763 Proclamation Line seemed not so temporary.

On the other hand, the colonies were especially pleased with the resignation of Lord Hillsborough and his replacement by the Earl of Dartmouth as Secretary of State for the Colonies. Dartmouth had been president of the board of the Eleazer Wheelock's Indian Charity School, which to show their respect was renamed Dartmouth. Colonists felt Dartmouth really understood how they differed from Great Britain. And so, in March, with a new Secretary in place, the Assembly of Pennsylvania petitioned the Crown for a repeal of the duty on tea. In July of 1772, so did Massachusetts, but the petitions were not shown to King George until June of 1773. He took no action and Parliament felt it should not act until the colonists submitted, and paid the duty on tea as required. The colonists did. But, instead of recognizing their submission, Parliament saw weakness, and passed the Tea Tax of April 1773, before the King ever saw the colonial petitions.

Mr. Adams had not been silent all this time, and continued to press people to boycott British tea—but they continued to drink it.

Finally, Sam Adams had time to speak with Rafe. They arranged to meet one afternoon at the *Intrepid*. The day was warm for spring. As they began to discuss the happenings in Boston and how Gabe was doing at Harvard, Rafe finally got up the courage to ask his question.

Rafe asked hesitantly, "Mr. Adams, I have heard and read a lot of what thee believeth, and I believe it too. But what I do not understand is why the Sons of Liberty in Boston focus only on British taxation and not about the problems of the poor." As he looked at Mr. Adams, he went on quickly, "I do not mean to insult thee sir, I would just like to understand."

Sam Adams looked deeply into Rafe's eyes. He saw no malice in them, so responded as truthfully to Rafe about Liberty as he had to Gabe about poverty. "Rafe, I feel I know you well. As well as I know Gabe or any man. So I am going to share my thoughts with you. I do not believe America will ever be free as long as we are a part of the British Empire. From the first, I believed that we should fight, not against taxation but for independence.

"I thought during the discussions at the Convention of 1768 that we had a chance for independence then. The Boston Caucus was ready and eager to turn the convention into a revolutionary government, but those in the countryside were not ready. We had no military to speak of, except the militia, and Britain would surely have fought us and we probably would have lost. And so, it wasn't time. But as I look around now, I do not think it will ever be time. If the colonies continue to argue amongst themselves there will not be an army to defend us and there will not be an *us* to defend.

"I know you and others are upset by the essays I write. They are full of inflammatory language, but I do not know how else to awaken the people of the country. Remember the journal entry where Crispus Attucks speaks of how different America is from England and Europe? That concept of limitless possibility should be enough for anyone to realize we cannot be self-reliant or have confidence in the future greatness of America as long as we are dependent. Britain, even now, has us locked out from the West and those brave ones who ignore the Proclamation of 1763 do so at their own peril.

"So, I alter the truth a bit. I hold rallies and celebrations of past wrongs and try to change the hearts and minds of the people. If I broadened the work to support the poor, the message would be weakened. It is only when we have freedom that we can become a country that has no poor.

"So, I preach for the return to an earlier and simpler way of life, where friend helps friend and neighbor aids neighbor, where the wealthy share with the poor and the merchant cooperates with the worker. My ideas are more radical than even my friends admit, so I am truly alone, even in the midst of a crowd. I guess what I do to help the poor is explain their rights to them, explain how they are being mistreated, giving words to the wordless. If I give them the little I have, they would only become dependent on me. I want to give them the self-respect and the anger necessary to act."

Rafe sat thoughtfully as Mr. Adams finished. Then Rafe spoke enthusiastically, "I too long for the days when there are no poor. I too long for the days of action. But I cannot be a part of the violence that often happens when the crowd gets together. Is there not a way to independence that does not involve violence?"

"I do not know, Rafe. I do not believe we can truly be free if we do not fight. I do not believe there is any reason for Parliament or the King to release us into self-government. The violence in the past came from demonstrations gone awry. It was never my intent to have Huchinson's home and papers destroyed. But when the legislature and petitions have failed, the people have only demonstrations to awaken those in power to their senses. Those who have led crowds into mobs and demonstrations into riots are in jail. Despite our current problems with taxes, I believe there are opportunities ahead where a point can be made without violence. I will keep you and Gabe informed. Crispus Attucks would want me to do so!" replied Sam Adams. And so he did.

Rafe kept track of all the events of the colony, sharing the events with Gabe, and together they looked for the right opportunity to act.

Throughout much of the spring of 1773, the British schooner *Gaspee* caused problems for smugglers; smuggling was a way to avoid British taxes and trade with other countries. When the schooner ran aground after a storm in June, colonials rescued the crew and burned the ship. Customs officials did their best to discover who had burned the ship but the local people were silent. Not only was there no one to testify, there was no one who would talk about the incident. The lines were being drawn between colonists and the British.

Great Britain's newest tactic was to propose a civil list of government officials. These officials would be paid a regular salary from the customhouse receipts, in effect buying their support and making them independent of the Massachusetts Legislature. On the list were Hutchinson and his relatives, and relatives of his in-laws, the Olivers, several of them holding more than one post. The Boston town meeting called for an investigation, and Hutchinson tried to stop it. Sam Adams proposed the town appoint a Committee of Correspondence to take the issue to others in the province. Along with this issue, they sent a list of all past problems with Parliament, and suggested that more problems were coming. In these Letters of Correspondence, Sam Adams explained the situation in Boston and began a conversation with other colonies that would unite them in action.

Hutchinson should have left well enough alone, but he did not. In January of 1773, he lectured the General Court, stating that Parliament had authority over American legislatures. In fact, he maintained, the colony charter was a financial document not a constitution. The colonists were like sailors in the ocean, miles from home but still subject to Parliament, and like the sailors they had chosen to be far from home. Parliament was the authority in the colonies, as it was in England, and the colonists should just submit, as they do in England.

Colonists responded that Parliament had no authority over the colonies. That the charter, whether a financial document or a constitution, gave the colonists the right to self-government. In fact, the mandate stated: "The laws of the colonies should be as much as possible, conformable in the spirit of them, to the principles and fundamental laws of the English constitution, its rights and statutes then being, and by no means to bind the colonies to a subjection to the supreme authority of the English Parliament … The several charters conveyed to the grantees, who should settle upon the territories therein granted, all the powers necessary to constitute them free and distinct states."

Next, King James I was quoted: "America was not annexed to the realm, and it was not fitting that Parliament should make laws for those countries." Therefore, if they were not annexed, then they are not part of the realm and not subject to the legislative authority of the kingdom. Only the citizens of England were subject to the authority of Parliament.

The Assembly charged Hutchinson as a tyrant who had approved all of the Parliamentary actions. By March of 1773, legislatures in several colonies had set up Committees of Correspondence and were sharing information about their colonies with each other.

Hutchinson kept getting in deeper and deeper. In June 1773, his letters were made public. While many of his letters showed his opposition to the acts of Parliament, the ones that were published showed his lack of respect for Massachusetts, and Boston in particular. The letters "complained about the radical faction in Boston, pleaded for an end to liberties, and called for troops to subdue the populace." The published letters of Lieutenant Governor Oliver were the most damning. He "recommended changes in the charter and arrest of the 'principal incendiaries.'" When their letters were presented to the General Court, Hutchinson and Oliver were impeached.

By fall, Committees of Correspondence were organized in all colonies, just in time for the latest of Britain's ploys. The East India Company was in trouble. To help her survive, the Tea Act passed by Parliament made the East India Company the sole provider of tea to the colonies. The colonies received notice by letter that tea would be duty free in August. On September 6th the real truth came out. The tea would be subject to the Townsend Duty, only the tax would be paid upon delivery to consignees. Those who accepted the British tea and sold it to other businessmen would add the tax to the price of the tea. The revenue of the tax would be used to fund the salaries of governors and judges in America.

By October 1773, handbills were printed that stated: "If we allow this tax then more taxes will follow. And, if the East India Company gets the tea monopoly, then there may be monopolies of all foreign commerce. As a result, all independent trade would disappear and Americans would be reduced to fur trappers and lumberjacks."

Americans reacted in various ways. Many American captains refused to let their ships be filled with tea cargo. Hutchinson requested that his sons be named consignees to enhance their business futures. In response, colonists in various ports threatened the consignees. In New York, pilots were threatened and refused to guide tea ships into the difficult harbor. No hand would unload the tea cargo, and there were threats made against anyone who would unload and store the tea. The consignees in New York, and later in Philadelphia, resigned.

In Boston, Governor Hutchinson gave full support to the consignees, and two of his sons were named agents. There were still British soldiers in the fort, Castle William, and ships-of-war in the harbor. The consignees were threatened but they spent their nights out of town away from crowds and mobs. For the people of Boston several things became clear.

Hutchinson had sons who were agents, and his friend Oliver was one of the consignees. Hutchinson and Oliver had continued to import British goods during the time of nonimportation, and so they were the enemy as much as the British Parliament.

1773

Road to Action

While colonists in New York and Philadelphia took action, colonists in Boston continued drinking their tea. Some smuggled tea, while others purchased it, supporting merchants who were willing to pay the duty. In fact, Boston imported over three thousand chests of tea under the Townsend Act. All this infuriated Sam Adams, who had argued that more taxes would come, and to support *any* tax was to allow for more taxes.

By November 1773, Boston was alone in not taking any real action against the Tea Act. In embarrassment, Boston finally acted. Consignees were ordered to appear at the Liberty Tree on November 3rd to resign. They did not appear and, in fact, were meeting just down the street. When this became known, the crowd that came to watch became a mob and rushed the building and pulled the doors off their hinges. The consignees made it to the second floor and hid behind a stout door. Eventually the mob left and the consignees walked home. On November 5th, a Town Meeting was held at Faneuil Hall to endorse the resolutions adopted by Philadelphia, announcing Boston's opposition to the importation of tea. The consignees continued to refuse to resign.

Rafe feared additional violence. In letters to Gabe, he fully explained the situation. It was Gabe's idea to peacefully dump the tea in Boston Harbor, if and when it arrived. With the help of the Sons of Liberty and with the blessings of Sam Adams, Gabe and Rafe finalized their plan. First, if and when the tea arrived, all legal means had to be actively attempted before the people acted. Second, if as a last resort it was decided to dump the tea in the harbor, there was to be no violence to anyone, for any reason, and there was to be no damage to the ship or to any other cargo. Third, no one was to pocket tea for themselves or profit financially in any way by their actions. Fourth, and most important, there would be no unruly mob bent on destruction, only silent watchers to a peaceful demonstration of the rights of citizens. Gabe and Rafe would stay in close contact, and Gabe would come home from Harvard for the event. In the meantime, Rafe would make all the arrangements in Boston.

Matters soon came to a head. Captain Haley and his ship arrived in Boston Harbor on November 17th, informing Boston that the British tea ships had sailed when he did. That night, rioters gathered outside the home of Richard Clark, one of the consignees. His sons were so frightened, one of them fired a gun out a second-floor window. At this, the crowd went mad and smashed everything on the first floor. The rioters eventually left. The consignees, now fully frightened, drafted a petition to the Governor and Council describing the insults and attacks, and stating that they feared destruction of cargo when the tea should arrive. They suggested turning the tea over to the Governor and Council. On November 27th, the Council, still at odds with Governor Hutchison, refused to act.

During this time period, Sam Adams and the Committee of Correspondence had not been idle. On November 22nd they invited the area towns of Roxbury, Dorchester, Brookline, Cambridge, and Charlestown to a meeting at Faneuil Hall. In the letter sent to the area towns, Adams had written: "Now brethren, we are reduced to this dilemma, either to sit down quiet under this and every other burden that our enemies shall see fit to lay upon us as good-natured slaves, or rise and resist this and every other plan laid for our destruction as becomes wise freemen. In this extremity we earnestly request your advice, and that you would give us the earliest intelligence of the sense your several towns have of the present gloomy situation of our affairs."

The conclusion reached at this meeting was if the East India Tea Company could not land the tea, the Company would ask for a repeal of the Tea Act. Rafe found this a logical conclusion and passed the information on to Gabe.

Now the consignees of the tea and the ship owners had a difficult problem. According to the Tea Act, if the tea were to be returned to England, then both the tea and the ship would be seized by the British.

On November 28, 1773, the first of the three tea ships arrived. The Captain of the *Dartmouth* was quickly made aware of the situation. Not wanting to lose his ship if the tea were returned to England, he willingly held off reporting to the customs officers, hoping for a solution. He legally had forty-eight hours before he had to report. But once the ship and cargo were registered, the ship had only twenty days to pay the duty or the ship and cargo could be seized for nonpayment.

A squad of twenty-five Sons of Liberty was placed on the wharf near the *Dartmouth* so no tea would be unloaded and no destruction would take place. On November 29, an unofficial Town Meeting was organized at Faneuil Hall, but the crowd was so large it moved to the Old South Meeting House. There the citizens of Boston resolved that the tea must be returned. The consignees felt helpless, fearing the loss of the price of the tea. They went first to the Town Council, who again refused to act, saying: "Let Hutchinson's relatives pay the price for trading with Britain." The consignees were then sent to the Justice of the Peace, who said he could not act to unload the tea as most of his militia members were also Sons of Liberty.

By now the agents had agreed to return the tea, but could not legally do so or they would lose the cargo and the ship. They proposed a compromise. They could not return the tea, but they would not interfere if the people sent it back, and they would make no attempt to unload the tea. They asked John Singleton Copley, a man trusted by both sides, to be mediator between the consignees and the town. Over five hundred townspeople attended a meeting to discuss the issue. This was not called a legal town meeting; so the city of Boston could not be held responsible for its actions. The meeting was peaceful and asked the questions: When is the duty due, upon arrival, when entered into the custom house, or when landed on the wharf?

The unfortunate answer was "upon arrival." The consignees and the owner of the *Dartmouth*, Francis Koch, tried hard to find another solution. Koch, who did not want to lose his ship, which he would if his captain sailed back to England with the tea, tried every avenue he could. Koch kept in close contact with Sam Adams, and reported to the mass meeting. The bottom line was Hutchinson would not budge. He felt the Bostonians had embarrassed him enough. If the ships had anchored near Castle William they could have unloaded the tea and returned easily to sea. This plan was foiled when the *Dartmouth* tied up at Griffin's Wharf.

This was one time Hutchinson felt he still had control. There were soldiers and officers at Castle William, and warships blocked the harbor, so no ship could leave without clearance. Hutchinson had no intention of giving clearance to any ship still loaded with tea.

By December 2nd the consignees in all other ports but Boston had resigned. The people of Boston did not discover until December 13th that the New York and Philadelphia consignees had given up all responsibility for the tea. By then, the tea ship *Eleanor* had docked, followed closely by the *Beaver*. All three tea ships were now docked at Griffin's Wharf, and the twenty-day limit was running out for the *Dartmouth*. By December 14th, the *Dartmouth* and *Eleanor* had unloaded what other cargo they could, and reloaded their ships with goods for England, but could not leave with the tea still onboard.

The *Dartmouth* requested clearance, but was put off until December 16th. The customs official, Harrison, could not grant the clearance because the tea had already been entered into the customs books by the pre-mentioned forty-eight-hour deadline. An appeal made to the colonial naval officers was denied. They could not grant clearance because they did not have the authority. A final appeal for clearance was made to Governor Hutchinson. He refused again.

When this was reported to the mass assembly, Sam Adams said, "This meeting can do nothing more to save the country." At this pre-arranged signal, people rose up yelling, "Hurrah for Griffins' Wharf!" and "Boston Harbor a teapot tonight!" and "The Mohawks are come, every man to his tent!"

Rafe and Gabe were already at the wharf waiting for the others to arrive. They had waited through the rain, and now that the rain had stopped the crowd came running. The evening was as bright as it could be from a quarter moon. The crowd that gathered had brought lanterns and stood silent, watching. The evening itself was quiet. No bird calls, no watchmen calling the hour, only the creak of block and tackle as the tea chests were raised from the hatches below deck and the "whack, whack" as tea chests were hatcheted open, the scrape of shovels against the deck, and whoosh as tea landed in the water. In three hours, the work was done.

Throughout the fall of 1773, fourteen-year-old Sarah had noticed the frequency with which Gabe and Rafe exchanged letters. She knew they were close, she also knew Rafe did not share all the letters from Gabe with the family. Rafe went out with *friends* several evenings a week. He was not out long, only a few hours, but it was unusual behavior for Rafe. Sarah brought up this change to her mother and father one evening.

Matthew and Charity smiled at each other and said, "Sarah, Rafe has celebrated his eighteenth birthday this summer. It is only natural that he be out a bit in the evenings with his friends. He works hard, and a few hours away now and then is a way to have fun. It is the way of young men. Rafe never comes home smelling of tobacco or alcohol, so what damage could he be doing to himself?"

Sarah nodded, and said she understood, but wondered to herself if Rafe were meeting with the Sons of Liberty and planning some action. So, she watched, listened to events of the time, and was aware of the problems the arrival of the tea ships might cause.

On that December night in 1773, Rafe had gone out again. Sarah was worried and could hold her thoughts in no longer. "Mother and Father, I think Rafe is getting into trouble tonight."

"Why do you believe that child?"

"Today is the day the decision needs to be made about the tea ship, and Rafe is gone. Yesterday when Rafe read us the letter from Gabe he hid the last page in his jacket so we didn't hear that. Rafe goes out at night and I do not think it is with friends. I think he is with the Sons of Liberty for he is gone the very nights they meet. And, I thought I heard Gabe's voice in the garden tonight. I kept waiting for him to come in, but he did not. I think that Gabe and Rafe are planning some action for Crispus Attucks, in remembrance of him," Sarah said breathlessly.

Charity and Matthew looked at each other, and then Matthew spoke. "You are probably right, Sarah. I have noticed whispered conversation between Rafe and Sam Adams, and more young men than usual seem to stop by the print shop lately." Looking at Charity, Matthew continued, "We did not ignore your earlier worries, Sarah, and we saw the furtive hiding of that last page of Gabe's letter. But we have to trust that we have raised you all well. The boys know what a Quaker is. They know that violence only begets more violence. Now, perhaps, tonight is the test of their beliefs. Your mother and I feel they will choose wisely."

Those in cabins by the harbor heard little but smashing and splashes. They saw the lights and decided locking doors was the better part of valor. In the morning, Luke, with a pregnant Jean, and their baby, along with John, Mary, Hope, Faith, and Lovey walked to the harbor. What they saw astonished them. During the night someone had filled the harbor with tea, tea chests, and broken crates. They could only wonder what that meant. In her heart, Hope knew that Rafe had been party to the event and prayed that he was safe.

In all the excitement of the day, little attention was paid to the schooner *Polly II*, as she slipped into port. The bronzed captain was the first ashore. He strode into Paul Elsener's office and caught Paul as he tripped in surprise. "Bryan! Bryan lad! We thought you were dead!"

"No, sir. As you can see, here I am. I lost the *Polly* in the storm, half the crew, and all her cargo."

"Lad, how did you get home?"

"On the *Polly II*. I couldn't come home empty-handed. Rosemary and I have great plans."

"Rosemary," Elsener said, slapping his forehead. "She's here, in Boston. She's only a few streets away. She and Polly have been working as housekeeper and maid to a local family."

"Where?"

Elsener pointed to the Anderson's.

"We'll talk later, Paul!" Bryan ran the few blocks to his wife.

Their excitement at reuniting as a family was louder and more laugh-filled than the joy after the work in the harbor that night. And the next day, the harbor was filled with a joy and awe that equaled that of Gabe, Rafe, and Sam Adams.

Seeing the crowd gather in the harbor after their captain left, the first mate and part of the crew decided to stay aboard to protect the cargo of the *Polly II*. They were to be given shares in the profits once the cargo was sold, and they had more than earned their shares.

While they protected the ship, Bryan was sitting before a fire, sharing his adventures with his wife and daughter. He explained that after the *Polly* had been hit by the storm, lost half the crew and half her cargo, she had limped into the bay of an uncharted island. After making what repairs they could, they set sail for a harbor. She barely made it, leaking so badly the crew could hardly keep up with the pumping. In order to make her seaworthy again, the *Polly* required almost total rebuilding. The captain sold what cargo remained to rebuild what he now called *Polly II*. He and what was left of his crew carried goods between islands until they had made enough to purchase another cargo to take home. Because of their hard work, and because of the dangers that lay ahead, the crew was promised shares in the profits.

Boston Harbor, a Teapot Tonight

On a cold night, in the middle of December, the docks were alive with "Mohawks," or those dressed like Mohawks, breaking open boxes and dumping the contents in the harbor. On shore, a silent crowd, some holding lanterns, watched these "Indians," and the quiet, peaceful act of rebellion. Three British ships had been boarded and their cargo of tea tossed into the water of Boston Harbor.

A little after nine o'clock in the evening, two Quaker brothers made their way home, their faces still marked from their rebellious actions. One brother was sixteen and attending Harvard, the other brother was eighteen and worked in the family print shop. They each had soot painted on their faces as though they were Mohawks, but that brave and proud people had long since been extinguished or forced further west.

"Yahoo! Hurrah for Griffin's Wharf!" said Gabriel as he did an Indian-style dance, hand to and from his mouth, his legs bending at the knees and stamping. "Everything was perfect! Even the crowd, who brought lanterns. Did thee hear the silence as we worked? Even O'Connor, who filled the lining of his coat with tea, was not hurt. The boys just stripped him of his coat and whacked him a bit and he took off running. But no one tried to stop him or really hurt him."

As Gabe stopped for breath, Rafael spoke quietly, "Yes, it was perfect. Three hours and the job done. It's only a little after nine now." Looking at his frenetic brother, Rafe continued pulling out a bit of cloth, "Why not stop and rest a moment before heading home? Thee will want to get the burnt cork off thy face anyway. Mother and Father may not be pleased at our actions."

"Was not it great at James Brewer's? We all got marked. I liked the Liberty boys who wore their hair like Mohawks; some even chose to paint their faces ..." Gabe just could not sit. He kept dancing, but when Rafe finally found two barrels together and seated himself, Gabe relented, though remained excitable and nervous.

"Look at the stars tonight. Have thee ever seen such beautiful stars? And there is the Big Dipper. Remember how to tell the time?" Rafe asked.

"Sure, I have not forgotten anything Tucks taught me. Thee looks for the stars across the handle of the Big Dipper, draws a line to the North Star, and with that star as the center of the clock, time becomes easy, if thee remembers the lines go counter-clockwise."

"He was a good friend."

"Yes, he was. And it was not right, not right at all ..." Gabe stood up and began to pace.

Rafe tried again to calm him. "He would have been proud of us tonight."

"Yes. That there was no violence ... that is what makes no sense of his death ..."

Rafe interrupted. "But thee know that was his choice. He said sometimes one has to act, even if ..."

"One would rather not. Being intrepid means ..."

"Being brave and adventurous, when others think thee are foolish," finished Rafe.

"I do not think he was foolish, I think he was a hero. I shall never forget him—ever!" Gabe said, nervously pacing.

"Thee should not forget him. I will not either, which is why tonight was so important."

"Right! After all the out-of-control mobs this needed to be the event that spoke to the Governor, and the King." Speaking more calmly, Gabe continued, "We are not simply an unruly, barbaric people. We are Englishmen, American Englishmen, and our words, our petitions, should be heard." Calmer now, Gabe sat down.

Rafe answered. "I do not think I could have been part of tonight if it had turned into a destructive event. What we did was truly remarkable. We escorted the customs officials ashore ..."

"When they did not want to leave!" Gabe smilingly interjected.

"Right. But there was no violence. No threats, really. They knew it made sense to leave when they saw the size of the crowd. I think they understood that this was different from other events."

"Sure, no tar and feathers. This time it was just 'Go ashore, and let us do what we have to do.'"

"I like that, 'Let us do what we have to do.' Adams and Otis, and even the ships' captains tried everything to enable the ships to leave and not unload the tea. Instead, just load the new cargo and take the tea back to England."

"Well, Governor Hutchinson was certainly given enough options to save face," Gabe added. "Why should we have to support the East India Tea Company, or pay for a war between France and England? Colonists did their share anyway, and lost many good men." More agitated now, Gabe continued, "New York, Charleston, and Philadelphia let the tea ships sail, but no, Hutchinson would not. He was more interested in enriching his sons or he would have found a way."

Rafe said, "Right. And if he were truly a supporter of the colonies, as he maintains, he would not have told the ships they could not leave without unloading the tea."

"And, if they unloaded the tea, then many in town would buy the tea and pay the tax. Well, we had a good plan ready if every attempt failed."

"I like that we had a plan ready. I think the organization prevented violence to crew and damage to ship and cargo from happening," Rafe said calmly.

"Right, the crew even stayed below. Ninety of us to handle the three ships, each of us knowing our stations, went to work. Some brought the tea crates up from the hold, some used block and tackle to raise the chests, others hatcheted the tea chests open, and me, I shoveled tea into the harbor."

"Thee were a sight, Gabe, shoveling like mad on the *Eleanor*, and others working just as hard on the *Beaver* and the *Dartmouth*. The tide was out, so some of us had to push the broken tea chests away from the ships to make room for the rest."

"I will not forget the crowd, Rafe. They were silent. Almost voiceless. I wondered if they were in awe of what we were doing or in awe over the destruction of their favorite beverage. I cannot imagine that coffee will ever be as popular as tea."

"It might," Rafe responded. "Maybe it will become an American beverage. Regardless, I hazard a guess many of us will be dumping tea out of our hair and shirtsleeves tomorrow. Tea was everywhere. I bet the harbor tastes like salty tea for a month."

"I wonder if the fish will like it," laughed Gabe. "Be thee in the mood to dump more tea crates into the harbor?"

"More crates? From where? Oh, thee means the *Intrepid*. I have not thought of our play boat for years. It is probably time for us, for thee, to move on. It has been two years since Crispus Attucks's death. Okay, let's go!"

Return to the *Intrepid*

The boys' thoughts were full of the past as they made their way to the stacked empty tea crates that had been the *Intrepid* and the sight of many conversations. In their eyes it would be remembered as their schoolroom for independence. Crispus Attucks had opened their eyes, and through Sam's essays, the eyes of the colonies.

They were not sure if Father and Mother would approve of their actions tonight. It was an act of open rebellion against the Crown, but it was also a nonviolent act of resistance. Rafe and Gabe hoped the King and Parliament would understand. The last thing the boys wanted was more troops and war. They felt it a good sign that Hutchinson had not acted this night. None of the soldiers from Castle Williams had appeared, and the warships had not re-acted beyond blocking the harbor. Maybe now the colonists would be listened to, maybe even a compromise could be worked out and America could have at least partial independence. They could run their own colonies, elect their own leaders, but still trade with England as before.

As Rafe looked at Gabe, he saw a tired sixteen-year-old boy still frail in mind and health. A boy who needed closure on this part of their lives.

Gabe spoke first. "I hated it when thee left school. Thee always made me feel protected."

"Thee knew I had to help Father in the print shop. It was not bad to begin work at twelve. That is the usual age for apprenticeship, and I was lucky, I got to learn from Father and Charles Cotter. Charles was a great teacher and stayed on that extra year for me, and for Father. So I was thirteen before the weight of the work fell on me. Thee know I love the work! I would not have enjoyed spending more time in school," Rafe replied.

"Yes, I know, but there I was, hanging about the harbor, playing on the ship, and talking to Tucks. Even after I returned to school, Father still had me spend time on the *Intrepid*, sketching and writing, while thee worked in the print shop and did my chores and thine. At least Charles came out ahead."

"Yes, with me gradually taking on the everyday work, Charles had time to learn the creative and more difficult aspects of printing. Father was pleased to be able to teach him more than the usual apprentice learned, and in return, Charles was able to help Father take on more work. And Charles was rewarded, he accepted a good job with one of the major printers and is doing very well! God rewards those who go beyond what is required.

"Besides, thee did not know it then, but thee too were doing valuable work for Father and for the cause. We always knew what ships were in harbor, and by thy sketches could guess the weight of the cargo. While thee were doing that, and by the way getting well, I was reading speeches, broadsheets, and newspapers as I set type and managed the press. I heard the talk between John Adams, Sam Adams, and Mr. Otis. And, I might add, thee were hearing from Tucks the news on the harbor, how the working man felt about the new taxes."

"Rafe, I guess I always felt my time in the harbor was useless. I always thought the *Intrepid* was built for me to play on because I was too young and sickly to do any real work."

"Thee are wrong about the *Intrepid*. I am sure part of its purpose was to give thee a place to be and a reason to be there, but Father had a strong lesson for us to learn, and I think that was the real reason he built it.

"You were to have sun and sea air, but where? Father said he thought immediately of old Mr. Gregson. His place in the harbor was at the end of a long wharf which butted up to a small hill. The wharf was seldom used. Father couldn't remember a recent time that any ship had come into his wharf, though Mr. Gregson spent each day in his small shed as though a ship might come.

"Father contacted him, and Mr. Gregson was willing to have you be there, but made it clear that he didn't want to spend time talking to a child though he would 'keep an eye out for the lad.'

"There were plenty of empty crates and boards around Gregson's Wharf and it was fun building the *Intrepid*. At first, I was only eleven and enjoyed the time alone with Father. The only negative note was that thee were too ill to be with us yet," Rafe said. "The tea crates were empty, so not too heavy, but by the time we got to the top deck I was exhausted. Father promised I would be able to play with thee after school for a time before my apprenticeship began, but I thought we had built the Intrepid just for thee. I soon learned I was wrong. Remember the shape of the 'ship'?"

Gabe nodded.

"Well, I could not figure out why we built it that way. The ship itself was built two crates deep so the boards weren't needed for support, but obviously served some purpose."

"Then Father had us lie down," Gabe added.

"Yes, until Father had us lie down in the space between crates on the first deck. I did not understand at first why he made us lie down, and said we could not move for two hours. The opening, a crate wide, deep and high, was tight quarters for the two of us, though it faced the sun and was pleasant at first."

"Yes, but those were the longest two hours I ever spent, despite the sun's warmth. I had only been out of the house a few times, and I was thrilled to spend some time with you," said Gabe. "I didn't understand why at the time, but the idea must have come to Father from Mr. Woolman's talk."

"Yes, I think so. Remember how I said I could not imagine what it must have been like to come over on a slave ship, stacked like cordwood, on shelves, unable to move? Well, that was Father's purpose to help us to understand, except we only had to spend two hours instead of weeks without moving."

Gabe said, "When thee had to relieve thyself, I wondered what we should do. Father said we were not to move no matter what, but I could not imagine he meant for thee to soil thy trousers."

"Right," Rafe continued. "But I think he was ready for any result. He trusted us to stay there; luckily I could go between the boards and not wet myself."

Gabe said, "But a slave would not have been so lucky. He would have had to wet and soil himself in addition to having to lie there more than two hours. Think of what it would have been like to lie in waste and not be able to move!"

Rafe added, "And be chained like an animal the whole time. Remember, people died on the way from Africa, and so thee could have been chained and lying next to a dead man. Imagine what it must have been like for a woman, or a child! No wonder some Africans jumped to their death when they had a chance to get up on deck. We were lucky. We are lucky. And we do not ever want to be slaves. Not in 1773. Not in any time. Not of anyone. Not even the British."

"Amen," Gabe said. "We are equal to any British soldier, to any Englishman, and should be treated as such, not as slaves whose hard work and earnings can be taken at will in taxes!"

"I think we made that point clearly tonight. There was no violence, no destruction of any cargo except the tea. They must understand now that we need be listened to, that our petitions must be regarded."

Gabe asked, "What I do not understand is why they had chosen this way to raise money for the war."

"That is a bit confusing for me too. In the past, when there had been a need, we taxed ourselves to raise the money. This time, they did not ask. They demanded. They did back down on some of the Townsend Act requirements, but not on tea. They must have thought it was a compromise, but if so, it was one in which we had no say. I think Sam Adams and Mr. Otis are right. The British do not see us as Englishmen living in this new land, but as something less, and as such, not deserving of respect. I would not be a slave."

Gabe interrupted, "Nor I. Tucks was one, and even though he had a kind master, there was no respect, no sense of equality; though without Tucks and his family, the farm would not have grown as it did. I remember what he said about his father being a prince in Africa ..." At this point Gabe began to break down.

Rafe, waited until Gabe regained control. "Come on," he said, "let us go dump the last of the tea crates."

As they approached the *Intrepid*, Gabe became stronger. Rafe asked, "Is there anything here we should keep?"

Gabe said thoughtfully, "I think I will keep the flag. The rest is British."

Both boys began tossing the empty crates in the water. They tossed in the extra crates forming the prow, the lookout point. They tossed in the next levels, keeping the boards used for the impressment deck, stacking them neatly. Finally, they tossed in the lowest level, where they had lain for two hours trying to experience what the slave passage might have been like. When they were done, they sat on the nearby barrels without speaking.

Gabe suddenly broke into tears. Rafe allowed him to sob and held his brother as he cried for Crispus Attucks. "He was a good friend to me, Rafe. I am so sorry to lose him, so sorry I do not think I can bear it."

"Gabe," Rafe replied, "thee hast not lost him. Thee cannot lose him. He is a part of thee, and me, and Sam Adams, and everyone else who longs for peace and a decent living and freedom. That is what he died for!"

"Oh, Rafe, I know all this, but my heart is breaking."

"Gabe, consider what we did tonight. We acted. We told the British we are not unruly monsters. We did all this without violence, without destruction. No one was injured, just some tea tossed into the harbor. Crispus Attucks, thy Tucks, would be proud of us."

As Gabe listened, his sobs eased. He released himself from his brother's arms and sat on a barrel quietly. After what seemed hours to Rafe, Gabe spoke again. "Thee are so very right, my brother, we did act as we said we would. Thy arrangement with Sam Adams was so perfect! Everything was perfect tonight—except Crispus Attucks was not here to see it."

"I think he was, Gabe. I feel him here, even without the *Intrepid*. If you are ready, let's go home."

"Yes, Rafe. I think thee are right, Tucks was here. And I have to begin again at Harvard and begin again my own work. Let's go home."

The next day, many wondered at the harbor. With the tide out, boats went out to break up the hills of tea which reached far into the harbor. As it turned out, Governor Hutchinson had been in Milton the night before, and was caught unaware. Hutchinson had believed that if the colonists could not return the tea, they would have no choice but to let it be unloaded and stored for nonpayment of duty. The twelve warships, with their two hundred and sixty guns within firing range of the town, were aware of the harbor activity but to act would mean firing on the town. Admiral Montagu considered action, then considered the massacre, and chose not to act. And, there were too few troops in Castle William to stop the "Mohawks."

John Adams wrote: "This is the most magnificent Movement of all, there is a Dignity, a Majesty, a Sublimity in this last Effort of the

Patriots that I greatly admire ... This Destruction of the Tea is so bold, so daring, so firm, *intrepid*, and inflexible, and it must have so important Consequences and so lasting, that I cannot but consider it as an Epoch in History."

It would have been a perfect tea party if England had understood. Maybe they did understand. Maybe they were unwilling to find a compromise, for their actions and words spoke loudly that there would be no independence for the Americans. Instead they passed the Coercive Acts, Intolerable Acts to the colonists. They closed the port of Boston until the tea was paid for. The Governor of Massachusetts would now appoint the Judges, and British officials accused of crimes would be sent to England for trial. And the worst, only one town meeting could be held per town, and only to elect town officials. No longer would the people of Boston be able to meet to decide the topics for the Assembly. Boston would not stand still for this, and so the road to war was laid, brick by brick.

For now, the boys felt they had acted for the best. Their parents understood. Sarah was proud of them and so thankful they were safe. Hope realized she loved Rafe, and prayed each night for her hero to love her. Gabe and Sarah were thrilled that Polly's father had come home safely.

Gabe and Rafe still had to work out their own demons. What *did* being a Quaker mean in an age of revolution? But now, they each felt the need to focus on truth, and to share that truth, as Sam Adams had said, *with anyone who would listen.*

Sam Adams expressed the thoughts of many as he wrote under the name Candidus: The liberties of our country are worth defending at all hazards. If we should suffer them to be wrested from us, millions yet unborn may be the miserable sharers in the event. Every step has been taken but one; and the last appeal would require prudence, unanimity and fortitude. America must herself, under God, work out her own salvation."

Looking at her children, Charity thought, 'As each of us must!'

Epilogue

Gabe completed his studies at Harvard. He wrote about the truths—poverty, unemployment, slavery, and independence. Gabe saw the *Declaration of Independence* signed. He applauded the lines, "We hold these truths to be self-evident, that all men are created equal and endowed by their creator with inalienable rights, that among these are life, liberty, and the pursuit of happiness." Crispus Attucks would have been proud of these words, but would have rightly said, he had heard them before and few took any action to make them reality.

Sarah fell in love with Charles Cotter, who had been her father's apprentice, and who became a lieutenant serving with Washington during the Revolutionary War. After the war, she and her husband would move to the Ohio River Valley and become farmers. Their home was always open to anyone in need.

After Father died, Mother continued to live with Rafe. Rafe maintained the print shop, and expanded it to two presses. He married Hope, who loved his mother as much as he did. They had two boys, Gabe and John. John was a sickly child and Rafe worried about him. But both boys were intelligent and eventually attended Harvard.

Gabe didn't marry for several years. Polly had moved away, and the thought of wife and family seemed a distraction to the work he was doing. They met again ten years after the return of the *Polly II*, their friendship rekindled, and love followed.

Rafe lived under the *Articles of Confederation* and then under the *Constitution*. He protested in print against ratification of the *Constitution*

without a *Bill of Rights*, and would have lost his business but for the intervention of an aging Sam Adams. Rafe often read from Gabe's journal,
and remarked how blessed Gabe had been.

Rafe and Crispus Attucks and Sam Adams and Father and Mother
and Sarah and Gabe had all looked forward with hope to a future of
peace and equality. But Rafe died knowing slavery, impressment of sailors, and poverty still existed, and that it might take a war, or several wars
to make things right. And like Father said, "Violence begets violence."

Rafe continually hoped for peace, and died praying for it.

Author's Note

The story you have read is true. Oh, Gabe, Rafe, and family are my creation, and their relationship with Sam Adams and Crispus Attucks is my creation, as are Uncle, and Mrs. Watson, and the young couple who lived in Tucks's cabin. But the story is true. Quakers and the champions of freedom for slaves, Benezet, Woolman, and others existed. There were Quakers who felt as the Bellsons, and Mrs. Watson was typical for her time, as were the stories Tucks told of the Middle Passage, King Philip's War, whaling, and the information he provided about ships. Unfortunately, the information on sadistic ship captains is also true.

I chose Crispus Attucks as a centerpiece because so little is known about him. We know he was killed at the Boston Massacre, that he was a runaway slave, and a mulatto. He might have been part Indian, his mother might have been Nancy Attucks, his father might have been Prince Younger who survived the Middle Passage, and Tucks might have gone to sea on a whaling ship.

After the massacre, Crispus Attucks was first identified as Michael Johnson. His actions at what has been called the Boston Massacre are so tied up with the economics of the time that the story seems real to me. There has been much written about the actions of crowds, but to put the blame on Sam Adams is to deny the ability of workers to think, or to understand how their situation worsened with each new tax and the arrival of soldiers.

The rebellious actions of wage workers, slaves, and sailors are ages old. In America, the rebellions began early. In Boston alone, seamen rioted twice in 1741 and twice more in 1745. The Knowles Riot in Boston in 1747 is typical of these riots: First, the crowds were composed of black and white laborers and seamen. Second, the crowds were protesting press gangs. Third, the crowds quickly rose in size, and while the riot may have begun with seamen, it quickly included all those disadvantaged in wages. And fourth, the riot began over a local issue—impressment—but extended to the larger issue of the rights of laborers, rights that governments were ignoring.

Rioting was not limited to Boston; but also happened in New York, Rhode Island, and other colonies. Some believe Sam Adams took his cue from those riots, and their reasoning, to develop his own thoughts on the rights of man.

I abhor the violence, but know from present times that when people have no choices, no way out, they will fire guns like Richardson, or become destructive, rioting mobs. Let us all learn from history, and from Matthew, that violence begets violence. May we all be intrepid seekers of truth.

A special thanks to: J.Y. Joyner Library at East Carolina University which gave me a place to research and write and whose helpful staff encouraged me; Ruth Graves who edited an early manuscript and asked many questions; Gail Chavenelle who reviewed a later manuscript; Patt Hopkins who helped me with punctuation; and Dianne Andersen who believed in me and in Gabe. The illustrations of Jason Parker brought the real Crispus Attucks to life for me. I would not have said "I am finished" without the careful editing of Mary Jo Zazueta.

A special thank you for excellent advice from— Dirk Hoerder, Professor Emeritus, Arizona State University (History), and author of *Crowd Action in Revolutionary Massachusetts: 1765-1780*—Irv Brendlinger, Professor, George Fox University and author of *Anthony Benezet: True Champion of the Slave*—and Eric Schultz, author of *King Philip's War*. I appreciate the time you spent on my manuscript!

Despite all the help, I accept responsibility for any errors I have missed and any changes I did not make.

For those of you who would like to know more, or would like to know my sources, I have included endnotes. I hope my interpretation of the events causes you, the reader, to realize that though much may change, much remains the same.

Endnotes

1767 TUCKS

Crispus Attucks http://en.wikipedia.org/wiki/Crispus_Attucks

Williams, George W., *History of the Negro Race in America, from 1619 to 1880, Negroes as Slaves, as Soldiers, and as Citizens*, G.P. Putnam's Sons, the Knickerbocker Press, New York and London, 1885.

Sailing Ships http://njscuba.net/artifacts/ship_sailing_ship.html.

SEAMEN

Gilje, Paul A., *Liberty on the Waterfront, American Maritime Culture in the Age of Revolution*, University of Pennsylvania Press, Philadelphia, 2004. Chapter 3, especially pages 72-74

Between the Devil and the Deep Blue Sea, Merchant Seamen, Pirates and the Anglo-American Maritime World, 1700-1750, by Marcus Rediker. Cambridge University Press, Cambridge 1987. Especially the Journal of James Fountaine.

AT HOME

Thomas, P.D. G., *British Politics and the Stamp Act Crisis*, Clarendon Press, Oxford, 1975.

Reese, William S., *The First Hundred Years of Printing in British North America: Printers and Collectors*, http://www.reeseco.com/papers/first100.htm.

Cremin, Lawrence A., *American Education: The Colonial Experience, 1607-1783*, Harper and Row, New York, 1970, pp. 388-395 and pp. 444-450.

Marten, James, editor *Children in Colonial America*, foreword by Philip J. Greven. New York University Press, New York and London, 2008, pp204-213

Foolscap: Sateren, Shelly Swanson, *Going to School in Colonial America*, Blue Earth Books, Mankato, Mnn. 2002, page 24

Apprenticeships, school day: *Ibid.*, pages 13-22

A PECULIAR PEOPLE

Wollman and Benzett: Drake, Thomas E., *Quakers and Slavery in America*, Yale University Press, 1950pp.48-67

Freedom of slaves: *Ibid.*, pp. 68-80

Jones, Rufus M., assisted by Isaac Sharpless and Amelia Gunnere, *Quakers in the American Colonies*, Macmillan & Co. Limited, London, 1911, pp. 28+

Society of Friends-Quakers http://mb-soft.com/believe/txc/quakers.htm Spring 2008

THE PRINCE

Op. Cit., Williams

INNER LIGHT

Quote: Morgan, Edmund S. and Morgan Helen M., *The Stamp Act Crisis, Prologue to Revolution*. Published for The Institute of Early American History and Culture at Williamsburg, Virginia, by The University of North Carolina Press, Chapel Hill,1963. Page 189

Anthony Benezet: Brendlinger, Irv, *Anthony Benezet: True Champion of the Slave*

http://wesley.nnu.edu/wesleyan_theology/theojrnl/31-35/32-1-7.htm
Philosophers and Divines, 1720-1789, #6. John Woolman
http://www.bartleby.com/225/0506.html
History: *Op. Cit.*, Drake, pages 50+
First Wollman quote: *Ibid.* page 56.
Op. Cit., Jones, assisted by Isaac Sharpless and Amelia Gunnere,
Op. Cit. Drake. page 58

SAILING SHIPS.

Crispus Attucks http://en.wikipedia.org/wiki/Crispus_Attucks
Sailing Ships http://njscuba.net/artifacts/ship_sailing_ship.html.

Tunis, Edwin, *Oars, Sails and Steam, A Picture Book of Ships*, The World Publishing Company, Cleveland and New York, 1952.

Storm description: *Op Cit*. Rediker. from the Journal of James Fountaine

SUMMER, 1767: IN THE PRINT SHOP

Op. Cit. Reese.

1768: TUCKS RETURNS

Dickinson information: Ferling, John, *A Leap in the Dark, The Struggle to Create the American Republic*, Oxford University Press, New York, 2003, "To Crush the Spirit of the Colonies," pages 69-71.

Adams information: *Ibid.* "To Crush the Spirit of the Colonies," pages 59-65.

Stout, Neil R., *The Royal Navy in America, 1760-1775*, Naval Institute Press: Annapolis, Maryland, 1973. Pages 110-147.

Society of Friends-Quakers http://mb-soft.com/believe/txc/quakers.htm Spring 2008

Fierce Feathers story: *Who are the Quakers* http://www.tudo.co..uk/quakers_craw/shell/contents/quakers/who_are_the_quakers/who_are_the_quakers.htm.

WAMPANOAG

Wampanoag Indian Fact Sheet
http:www.geocities.com/bigorrin/wampanoag_kids.htm Spring, 2008
Wampanoag (tribe) http://en.wikipedia.org/wiki/Wampanoag Spring 2008

Ways the Puritans got land: Schultz, Eric B. and Michael J. Tougias, *King Philip's War*, The Countryman Press, Woodstock, Vermont, 1999, page 19.

Wigwam burning: Hall-Quest, Olga *"Epilogue" Flames Over New England*, E. P. Dutton and Company, Inc., New York, 1967 pages 211

Quote on Philip: *Op. Cit.* Schultz and Tougias, page 33

Loss of Freedom: *Ibid.* page 77.

WORDS AND CHANGE

Samuel Adams; *Circular Letter from the Massachusetts House of Representatives to the Speakers of other Houses of Representatives Pro of Massachusetts Bay.*
http://www.historicaldocuments.com/SamuelAdamsCircularLetter.htm. Spring, 2008

Zobel, Hiller B., *The Boston Massacre*, W.W. Norton & Company, Inc., New York, 1970, pp. 69-86

Hutchinson' Attitude: Fradin, Dennis Brindell, *Samuel Adams: The Father of American Independence*, Clarion Books, New York, 1998, page 61

LEVIATHAN

Quote: Harlow, Ralph Volney, *Samuel Adams: Promoter of the American Revolution, a Study in Psychology and Politics*, Octagon Books, a Division of Farrar, Straus and Giroux, New York, 1975. Pages 140-141

Whitehead, Hal, *Sperm Whales*, University of Chicago Press, Chicago, 2003. Prologue pp. xix-xxiii and Chapter 5 especially pp. 184-193

Dolin, Eric Jay, *Leviathan: the History of Whaling in America*, W.W. Norton & Company, New York, 2007, pp. 76-96.

ROSES AND THISTLES

Op. Cit. Zobel, pp. 87-112

1769: UNREST

Op. Cit. Gilje, Pages 104-105

Miller, John C., *Sam Adams: Pioneer in Propaganda*, Little, Brown, and Company, Boston, 1936. Pages 171-173

Adams Journal: *Ibid.* pages 174-176

Hutchinson on soldiers: *Ibid.* page 176

Letters from a Farmer: *Op. Cit.*, Ferling, p.70

Bernard Leaving: *Op. Cit.* Miller p. 176

1770: JACK TAR

Rope-making Step-by-step

http://www.rope-maker.com/makingrope.html. Spring, 2008

Colonial Living, written and illustrated by Edwin Tunis, The World Publishing Company, Cleveland and New York, 1957, pages 124-125.

Rope Walk by Joseph Mussulman.

http://www.lewis-clark.org/content/content-article.asp?ArticleID=1796. Spring, 2008

Sam Adams-Mysteries of Government

http://www.historicaldocuments.com/SamAdamsMysteriesofGovernment.htm

Rope Walk: *Op. Cit.* Zobel, p.47

Unemployment: Lemisch, Jesse, Jack Tar vs. John Bull, *The role of New York's Seamen in Precipitating the Revolution,* Garland Publishing, New York and London, 1997, pp. 51-56, 90-91, 125

1770: LOBSTERBACKS, YOU DO NOT DARE FIRE!

Massacre: Hoerder, Dirk, *Crowd Action in Revolutionary Massachusetts: 1765-1780*, Academic Press, Harcourt Brace Javanovich, New York, 1977.. Pages223-230
Massacre: *Op. Cit.*, Ferling, pp. 74-77
Massacre: *Op.Cit.* Zobel, pp. 273-292
Preston: *Ibid*. p. 199

UNCLE

Crispus leads sailors: *Op. Cit.* Miller, page 180
Patrick Carr: *Ibid*. Miller, page 189
Soldiers Firing: Puls, Mark, *Samuel Adams: Father of the American Revolution*. Palgrave, Macmillan, New York, 2006, page 109

THE RIFT

Prelude to Revolution 1763-1775
http://www.historyplace.com/unitedstates/revolution/rev-prel.htm
English Colonial Era 1700-1763
http://www.historyplace.com/unitedstates/revolution/rev-col.htm

OCTOBER 1770: THE TRIAL

Patrick Carr: *Op. Cit.* Miller, page 189
Soldiers Firing: *Op. Cit.* Puls, page 109
Op. Cit. Hoerder.
Otis: *Op. Cit.* Puls, p. 97
Now brethren quote: *Op. Cit.* Fradin, p. 77.

MOTHER AND SARAH

Gundersen, Joan R., *To Be Useful to the World*, University of North Carolina Press, Chapel Hill, 2006. Chapter 2.
Berkin, Carol, *Revolutionary Mothers, Women in the Struggle for America's Independence*, Alfred A Knopf, New York, 2005.
Poverty: *Op. Cit.*, Ferling, p. 96
Holliday, Carl, *Women's Life in Colonial Days*, Cornhill Publishing Company, Boston, 1922
Collins, Gail, *American Women: Four Hundred years of Dolls, Drudges, Helpmates, and Heroines*, Harper Collin's Publishing, New York, 2003.
Boorstin, Daniel, *The Americans: The Colonial Experience*, Random House, New York, 1958.

SAM ADAMS

Samuel Adams, the Rights of the Colonists
http://www.usconstitution.com/RightsoftheColonists.htm. Spring 2008, page 3 of 6
Sam as a child: *Op. Cit*. Fradin, pages 2,3,6.
Op. Cit. Puls p.31
Egalitarian Society, *Op. Cit.* Ferling, p.62
Land Bank: *Ibid*. pp. 59-60
Economics: *Op. Cit*. Countryman p. 78
Dream: *Op. Cit*. Fradin, page 44.

THE SONS OF LIBERTY

History: *Op. Cit.* Countryman, pages 98-104

Barre quote: *Op. Cit.* Puls, page 30

Carriages quote: Raphael, Ray, *A People's History of the American Revolution*, Perennial, Harper Collins, New York, 2001, page 17.

Sam Adams: *Op. Cit.* Harlow p. 139

Actions and the Irish, Howell, Colin, and Richard Twomey, editors, "The Many-Headed Hydra: Sailors, Slaves and the Atlantic Working Class in the Eighteenth Century, pages 11-36, *Jack Tar in History: essays in the History of Maritime Life and Labour*, Acadensis Press, Fredericton, N.B. 1991. Pp.25-28

Parliament's authority, *Op. Cit.* Puls, pp. 134-136.

Governor Bernard, *Ibid.* Puls, p. 96

REFLECTION: DEEPER AND DEEPER

Hutchinson lecture and colonial response: *Ibid.* Puls, pp. 135-136

Hutchinson letters: *Ibid.* p.133 and 137 and *Op.Cit.*, Ferling p. 97

Tea Party events: Op.Cit, Puls. pp. 141-147 and Labaree, Benjamin Woods, *The Boston Tea Party*, Oxford University Press, New York, 1964,

1773: ROAD TO ACTION

Sam Adams-Mysteries of Government

http://www.historicaldocuments.com/SamAdamsMysteriesofGovernment.htm

Gaspee: *Op. Cit.* Puls page 130

Monopolies: Langguth, A. J., *Patriots: The Men Who Started the American Revolution*, A Touchstone Book, Simon and Schuster, New York, 1988. p.174

DECEMBER, 1773: BOSTON HARBOR, A TEA-POT TONIGHT

Op. Cit. Labaree pages 126-145

Op. Cit. Ferling, pages 103-108

RETURN TO THE INTREPID: DECEMBER 16, 1773

Op. Cit. Puls pp. 113-115

John Adams quote: *Op. Cit.*, Ferling, p. 107

Coercive Acts: *Op. Cit.* , Ferling, p. 107.

AUTHOR'S NOTE

"The Many-Headed Hydra: Sailors, Slaves and the Atlantic Working Class in the Eighteenth Century, by Peter Linebaugh and Marcus Rediker, pages 11-36, *Jack Tar in History: essays in the History of Maritime Life and Labour*, edited by Colin Howell and Richard Twomey, Acadensis Press, Fredericton, N.B. 1991.

About the Author

KATHERINE V. STEVENS is a poet, photographer, author, and retired high school teacher of English and history. She is also the facilitator of Brush Creek Writers in Hillman, Michigan.

She earned a BS in English/History from the University of Dubuque and an MA in English at the Bread Loaf School of English, Middlebury College.

Katherine resides in Northern Michigan with her ninety-three-year-young mother, who has permission to shovel snow.

You can contact Katherine via her website: chickadeehillinc.com, on Facebook, and her two blogs:

mysistersgardensite@blogspot.com

Thisisthemessage@blogspot.com (religious)